Puppy + Prey

Puppy + Prey

Trevin Thomas

authorHOUSE®

AuthorHouse™
1663 Liberty Drive
Bloomington, IN 47403
www.authorhouse.com
Phone: 1 (800) 839-8640

Published by AuthorHouse 01/27/2015

ISBN: 978-1-4969-6574-5 (sc)
ISBN: 978-1-4969-6573-8 (e)

Library of Congress Control Number: 2015900961

CHAPTER ONE

"You mean...in dogs years?"

Serving others can feel like slavery, without the proper compensation. Sometimes a simple reward suffices, but often a lack of gratitude or respect will cause people to crack. Slaves will happily work without pay, if they live in luxury like beloved pets, though paid workers can sink into despair despite their many opportunities. No one sacrifices anything without expecting something in return, whether that's food, money, protection, satisfaction, or love. Without compensation for their efforts, humans are more prone to depression, desperation, and impulsive decisions.

I'm not paid enough for this, thought Ken Inumura.

Ken, already stressed from a late dinner rush, impatiently listened to a guest complain about his steak. Resisting the urge to slap the man's fat, bald, tattooed head, he stood at the plush, burgundy booth grinning like a jackass, folding his hands and bowing in apology.

"Yes, it does look medium-rare to me," Ken said, contrary to his contrite smile.

The man's inked scalp bloomed red.

"Are you mocking me, you little shit?" He scooped a wine bottle off his table and tilted it back, growling when he realized it was empty.

"Please, sir, there are kids here." Ken motioned down the aisle.

Two booths over, a small girl nibbled on a crispy chicken breast like a squirrel, with buttery sauce dripping down her fingers. Her bushy tail brushed crumbs off of her seat, as she savoured her meaty treat. The fat man noticed her extra appendage, and he nearly spat on the floor in disgust.

"A *mod*? You serve those mutts here, too?"

"Everyone is welcome at À La Mod," said Ken. "Besides, we are a mod themed restaurant..."

"You know, I've had just about enough of your lip, boy. Where's your manager?"

"I'll get her for you," Ken said eagerly. In his haste to end the unpleasant interaction, he almost started jogging back to the kitchen. "Er, would you like me to make you another steak, sir?"

"Yes, I would," said the guest, but as Ken reached for his plate, he smacked his hand, grabbed his fork and knife, and stole a bite. "And make sure it's cooked properly next time," he said, stuffing another hunk of beef into his full mouth, "or I swear I'll get you fired."

Ken's fake smile melted into a scowl, but rather than pick a fight with an apparent thug in the middle of the crowded restaurant, he clenched his fists and left the man to enjoy his complementary meal. He stormed through the kitchen door, too irritated to bother looking through the window, and slammed straight into one of the servers.

"Whoa!" Ken gripped the boy's shoulders, saving him from a fall. "Sorry, Max."

Fortunately the boy wasn't carrying any plates. Max flashed a cute smile, rubbing the spot where the door hit him—right beside one of his floppy ears. The mod looked about twelve and wore a tuxedo. He was also covered in curly golden hair, except for his face, though his nose was darker than the rest of it, almost black, as if he'd suffered frostbite.

"Don't worry, that was my fault," said Ken. "You okay, buddy?"

Max nodded, gave the thumbs up, and bounded into the dining room.

Ken exhaled and went to find his manager, slowly, to admire the view on the way. For servers, the dress code at À La Mod included a tail, floppy or pointed ears, fur, and in the case of the women, a maid uniform. Shapely blonde and brunette legs stretched out from under frilly skirts, fluffy breasts threatened to spill over their cups, and everywhere Ken's eyes roamed, they found ribbons and lace.

In his white chef's clothes, Ken appeared dull by comparison, with his totally regular almond skin and black hair. His one notable feature, a pointlessly short ponytail that more closely resembled a puppy tail, distinguished him from the other human cooks, yet he felt something like envy for the male mod servers.

He noticed the way their tuxes bulged and their silken manes flowed as they strut throughout the restaurant, and he noticed the way women noticed. He also noticed the pretty redhead bending over to retrieve a fallen spoon. Distracted, he stumbled face first into a pair of warm pillows. A rough cuff to his head forced his eyes shut.

"Watch it, Ken!" a woman hissed, before sighing. "You know, if you wanna confess your love for me, there're better ways to do it."

Ken opened his eyes to find himself peering down a valley of flesh. Startled and embarrassed, he leaped back, tilting his head up to meet the tall woman's fierce gaze. She sneered down at him, hands on her hips. An untamed tangle of orange hair spiraled around her pouty face like flames.

"S-sorry, Sis. I—"

Suddenly she snatched him up and squeezed him into a headlock, crushing his skull between her hard bicep and her soft body.

"How many times have I told you not to call me that at work, huh?"

"It just slipped out!" Ken gurgled, thrashing like a mouse under a cat's paw. "I didn't mean it!"

"What was that?" She increased the pressure. "I didn't mean it...?"

"*Trish*! I didn't mean it, Trish!"

Trish finally released Ken. He scrambled away, pressing gently on his head, as if sculpting it back into its proper shape.

"Damn it..." he moaned, fixing his tiny ponytail. "What's wrong with you?"

"Oh, hush," Trish said, blushing for some reason. "I could've killed you if I tried, so quit crying."

Ken only sighed, knowing she might actually murder him if he called her a bitch, or an ape, or any of the other insults on his tongue. "Anyway, table eight called for the manager, so get going."

"Huh? What'd you do this time?"

"Nothing. The guy's an asshole, you'll see. Oh, and if he asks for something to drink, I cut him off. He's already finished two bottles, and who knows what else he had before coming here."

Trish grunted in aggravation. "Whatever. I'll handle it. Just get back on the grill."

Ken shuffled to his station beside the other cooks, grumbling when he saw the new tickets that had sprung up while he dealt with the drunk thug. Hoping other guests could stomach minor discrepancies of red and pink, he focused mainly on seasoning and searing the thug's steak, carefully counting the seconds it spent sizzling.

Halfway through this process, Ken heard Trish shout from the dining room:

"You've already eaten half! Pay up, or get the fuck out!"

He chuckled, shaking his head. Regulars might have expected these sorts of outbursts from Trish and continued eating, but Ken could only imagine how shocked the man looked as she towered over him, one hand ready to yank his plate away, the other balled into a fist.

The thug must've decided to pay, because Trish stomped back into the kitchen empty-handed, swearing under her breath. She marched straight up to Ken, threw back her head, then spit on his second steak.

"Table eleven has a birthday," Trish said nonchalantly. "When you're finished up here, grab a dessert and go sing."

"But—"

"Mods can't talk, and I'm sure as hell not singing. Hop to it!" With that, she patted his shoulder and strut off, leaving him to gawk at the frothing glob of mucus she left on the grill.

"But...that wasn't his steak." Ken sighed, tossing the soiled beef into the trash.

After plating the final dish on his tickets, Ken placed it under the heat lamps, grabbed a slice of chocolate cake from the fridge, and headed for table eleven. In case they saw him approaching, he feigned excitement along the way, but when he realized whose birthday it was, he genuinely smiled.

The little girl beamed up at him, her long tongue resting on her lip, while her owner finished wiping down her buttery fingers with a napkin. Ken set the cake down in front of her, and after she cautiously sniffed it, her tail happily thumped against her seat, and she clapped her hands.

Too cute! Ken thought, clearing his throat.

"Happy birthday! And what's your name, honey?"

"Honey, actually," her owner chuckled, a plain middle-aged man. "She's eighteen today."

"Eighteen?" Ken blinked at the girl, as she sipped at her wine. "You mean...in dog years?"

"Sorry," the man laughed again. "It can come as a bit of a shock to some people, but they don't call them mods for nothing, right? I had her growth capped, so she'll stay my sweet little girl forever. Wonderful, isn't it? Genetic modification truly is a miracle..."

Ken hesitated, inadvertently staring at the girl. She drained her wine and picked up her cake, nibbling off the frosting and giggling.

Her owner sighed. "I just wish she'd use her fork..."

Suddenly a harsh bang and the distinct clattering of dishes cut the nearby chatter, and gasps rippled behind Ken. Whimpering breached the sea of silence, followed by a belligerent voice:

"So, that hair's not yours, huh? Why don't you take a closer look, mutt?"

Ken spun, and the second his brain registered Max face down in food, he dashed to his rescue, ripping the thug's hand off his head.

"What do you think you're doing, you—!?"

A chunky fist smashed his gut, dropping Ken to his knees. Paralyzed, he tried to chew him out, but all he could manage was a choked, "Bastard..."

"Don't put your hands on me, punk-ass," the thug spat, sitting smugly in his booth. "Honestly, I've never had such poor service. But that's what you get with a bunch of retarded slaves."

Ken attempted to retort, but his lungs hadn't filled yet. Meanwhile, Max cleaned his face with the handkerchief from his breast pocket. Blood from his nose mixed with sauce from the steak.

"Whatever you paid for him, it wasn't worth it," said the thug.

"Max is a good kid," croaked Ken. "He was just doing his job."

"Job?" the thug snorted. "Last I checked, you get paid for a job. Does he work for treats? A cage to sleep in at night? It's thanks to little *shits* like him that I can't find any work nowadays. But I get it; why pay a real man when you can get a half dog to do it for free? I swear, this whole country's going to shit because of these fucking mutts."

"Shut up," Ken growled, rising to his feet. "Just shut your mouth! What the hell do you know, anyway? Max is here every day, busting his ass for ungrateful assholes like you! He never sees a cent, but at least he pulls his weight. How do you make your living, huh? Selling drugs? Stealing? And you blame him for this country going to shit? If he's a mutt, then you're even lower than a dog."

"What the fuck did you say!?"

The thug launched out of his seat, literally butting heads with Ken. Ken didn't budge, despite the throbbing ache drilling above his eyebrow. The two men glared head-to-head, seething—

"ENOUGH!" Trish bellowed, making them flinch apart. "You," she stabbed her finger at Ken, "meet me out back. And *you*," she pointed to the thug, "fuck off. Nobody treats my pup that way."

The thug scoffed. "Are you this blond bitch's master?" he asked, motioning to Max.

"I wasn't talking about him," Trish said, cracking her knuckles.

Ken palmed his own face, as the thug erupted in coarse laughter. "Whatever, lady," he said, pushing past Trish and heading for the front door. "I'm done with this dump, anyway. Thanks for the free booze, fuckers!" Moments later, a motorcycle engine roared, gradually fading into the distance.

Trish turned to berate Ken, but he somehow slipped by her like some morose ghost, dragging his feet and rubbing his temples. Instead she turned to Max and pet his curly head, before addressing the flustered customers.

"All right, people, the fight's been cancelled. Eat, eat!"

At her command, the familiar clacking of steel on plates returned. A surge of restless gossip chased Trish as she lead Max to the staff washroom, careful not to let his blood drip on the floor.

After a while, she escaped the stuffy kitchen through the backdoor, inhaling the humid night air. The sky loomed starless above, its radiance overpowered by streetlamps, digital billboards, and the luminous logos adorning sleek glass skyscrapers. Ken sat slouched on the nearby stairs, gloomy in contrast. She leaned against the railing beside him and ignited a cigarette.

"You cooled off yet?" she asked.

"Why are we out here?" he sulked. "Am I in trouble or something?"

"Trouble?" Trish chuckled, sucking on her cigarette. "Of course not. Hell, I say you should've hit the guy. I just thought you could use a break."

"Oh," said Ken. "Thanks, I guess."

"Why're you being such a baby right now? Is it because Max got a little bloody nose? He's fine. I cleaned him up, and he's already back to work."

"It's not that. That guy in there was just so..."

"Let it go. Any asshole who would hurt a sweet boy like Max isn't worth losing sleep over. You'll probably never see him again, anyway."

"Not him," said Ken. "The older guy, with the little girl."

"What girl? The birthday girl?"

"Yeah. Her owner said he had her modified so she'll never grow up. She'll just stay a little kid, never knowing any better."

Trish exhaled a stream of smoke. "So?"

"So?" Ken snapped, swiveling. "*Eighteen*, Trish. She's eighteen years old. She looked so happy, too, like she was perfectly fine being his pet forever. Doesn't it bother you knowing that she'll never live her own life, never be free? I mean, her entire existence is just to be some old man's...*lapdog*."

Before responding, Trish dragged deeply on her cigarette, as if it helped her think. "That's just the way mods work, Ken. U-GeneTech cooks them to order, they're pets until they're about Max's age, and then they float around from owner to owner and job to menial job until they die. The rest of the world demanded an end to human slavery, and they're just the solution we have to live with now. Anyway, I don't hear you complaining about those waitresses you drool over all day."

"They're different," Ken stated defensively. "They might be slaves now, but if they were free, I'm sure they could live on their own."

"I doubt it. They'd never survive without humans. They're stupid and obedient on purpose. Leave one alone long enough, and it'll sleep in a corner until you give it a command. If you ask me, they're just slightly smarter dogs with hands."

"You're wrong," Ken said, rising from the steps and locking eyes with Trish. "They're human, just like me and you. They just need someone to lift them up, you know? Someone to teach them and give them some support. Weren't you the one saying you'd start paying them if you owned this place?"

"Not with money. What would they even do with it? I just think they should get some sort of reward, that's all. Not just somewhere to sleep and enough to eat, but...I don't know, treats or presents or something." She dumped her ashes over the railing. "Anyway, I don't own this place or those mods. They're company property, so it doesn't really matter what I think, does it?"

"Of course it matters," said Ken, leaning against the wall across from Trish. "You know what it's like to live like a dog, working and waiting for nothing. That freedom we felt when we finally ran away from the orphanage... Don't you want that for those people in there?"

Trish took another puff. "They're not *people*, Ken. The sooner you cope with that, the better. Besides, I certainly didn't feel free, working at twelve to support your ass."

"You know what I meant," Ken said, folding his arms.

"Why do you suddenly care so much about mods, anyway? Pretty soon, you won't even have to worry about them anymore."

"Huh?"

"*Huh?*" Trish mocked him. "What do you mean, *huh?* It's illegal to own mods anywhere else, and aren't you leaving the country soon?"

"That was the plan, but..."

"But...?"

"I dunno. I guess I feel like I'd be ignoring the problem or something, like I'd be abandoning all the mods if I left, you know?" Ken exhaled. "That sounds pretty dumb, right? What could I do for them, anyway? That said, the kind of house I want is pretty expensive. Maybe it'd be best if I stayed. I mean, I've been saving up for a few years, and I think I know where I want to move, but—"

Trish laughed inexplicably. "Say no more. I get it. You don't want to leave me behind, eh?"

"W-what?" Ken stammered, turning away and turning red. "No. It's a huge decision, that's all. I mean, I'd still miss you. I care about you, obviously, I just—"

Trish gripped his shoulder firmly, not hard enough to hurt him, but tight enough to convey her concealed feelings.

"Relax. I was teasing," she smiled. A breeze tousled her orange tangles. Ken rarely considered it, but with her smouldering green eyes and full feminine figure, Trish was quite beautiful. "It's been a pretty rough shift. Why don't you take the rest of the night off, all right? I'll cover for you."

Ken paused briefly, then nodded. "Yeah... Thanks, Sis."

She might've punched him, had they not been alone. "No problem," she said, stomping out her cigarette. "Just hang around for a bit, okay? I'll cook you something up to take home."

"Okay," Ken agreed, settling into the wall, as Trish ducked inside. Somehow, she returned less than a minute later with a steaming foam box.

"Here," she grunted, shoving the mystery meal into his hands. "That should fill you up."

You stole this from under the heat lamps, didn't you? Ken thought, accepting her gift anyway. "Sure. Thanks... I'll see you soon, I guess."

"Sure thing," said Trish. "Have a safe walk home, kiddo."

Kiddo? Ken thought, setting off. *I know you raised me for a bit, but we're only three years apart. Honestly...*

Ken spent much of his walk home mentally grumbling about her last remark, too distracted to appreciate the luminous splendor of the city. Personal vehicles like cars shared the wide streets with mass transit pods, which zoomed at dizzying speeds on rails. On major roads, citizens could use kiosks to call for smaller pods to taxi them to specific destinations for a high fee.

Ken stayed content with walking for free.

He lived less than twenty minutes from work, and he stopped riding bikes when thieves kept stealing them.

He only hopped in a pod when running late, but he was in no rush to race home to an old apartment complex composed of crumbling bricks. The recognized historical building jarred with the glossy city, like a festering pimple on the face of a fashion model. Unlike modern apartments, it lacked even basic security features like electric fences and keypads, but rent cost practically nothing, allowing Ken to quickly accrue cash for a better life elsewhere.

As he passed the alley, approaching the rusting front gate to his building, Ken suddenly heard a rough gurgling noise, like a spluttering lawnmower. Curiosity gripped him, pulling him toward the raspy sound. He snuck into the narrow lane, wary of disturbing whatever lurked within the shadows, and what he found stopped his heart for one horrifying second.

A naked woman sat slumped against a dumpster, panting, as she tore green fluff off of mouldy bread. The furry chunks fell in the glistening goo oozing from her gashes, swelling to soggy red blobs in her blood. Through her choppy black hair, her icy blue eyes found Ken. She dropped her bread and growled, crawling under a patch of moonlight.

Black and white fur blanketed her lean body, and her face was pale, except for her dark nose and lips. Ken recognized the colouring. *A husky, or malamute. Maybe even a wolf.* He occupied himself with thoughts like these to distract himself from his fear. She bared her teeth, and her mouth looked large enough to swallow his hand, and her claws clicked against the concrete with every stalking step.

"Y-You hungry?" Ken asked, opening his foam container. The smell of charred beef and fried potatoes mingled with the sickly scent of blood. He took a single potato wedge and held it out for the woman. "I'm not going to hurt you. You obviously need help, so just take it. Here..."

She pounced.

Her teeth grazed his finger, and she might have clamped down and ripped it off if she hadn't yelped in pain and collapsed, gripping her gashed leg. Ken tossed his food aside and rushed to help. She screamed to scare him, thrashing, but her cries faded into whimpers, and she lost consciousness.

Once he could safely reach her, Ken stripped down to his undershirt and wrapped her in his chef's jacket like a blanket. He cradled her dripping body, carried her to the nearest transit kiosk, and called for a pod to U-GeneTech General, a hospital that specialized in mods. She slept during the whole trip, her blood and ferocity drained. As medical staff carted her into surgery, Ken could only pray in the lobby, but even after her emergency operation was successful, he couldn't stop worrying.

"How could I not worry?" Ken asked her surgeon, pacing by her hospital bed while she rested. One of her bare legs peeked out from her covers. Pink tracks cut through her fur like worms, but they seemed no worse than the burns he sometimes received at work. Doctors sealed her wounds using extreme heat and gummy blue gel—another miracle courtesy of U-GeneTech—to accelerate healing. Ken couldn't comprehend it, but if it meant a quick, painless recovery for her, he couldn't question it. "I know she's not mine, but..." he tailed away. "Who could've done that to her?"

"Her owner, most likely," said the surgeon. "She has scarring from electrical burns. It's not uncommon for mod owners to use altered shock collars if they can't control them with leashes. Hair loss on her wrists and ankles suggests she was shackled for long periods of time. The scratches in her leg were deep and bizarre, maybe done by some sort of trap to stop her from running away, and who knows how long she's been on the streets. The only good news is she doesn't have any diseases."

Ken's fists clenched so tight his bones creaked, but he listened intently, unable to ignore the woman's anguished history. He listened out of some odd sense of respect, acknowledging her life.

"But the worst part is she's unregistered," said the surgeon. "No tag or tattoo, not even a collar. Her blood isn't in the database, either, meaning someone bred her illegally, the natural way."

"Why is that bad?"

"Well, we can keep her in our shelter next door, but whoever mistreated her might just find her again and take her back. Without knowing who bought or sold her, we can't guarantee her safety."

Ken couldn't believe what he was about to say, but he couldn't bear the thought of her owner, or anybody else, causing her any more pain. He wouldn't allow it, not if he could change her fate.

"What if I adopt her?" he asked. "Here. Tonight."

The surgeon looked incredulous. "If you register her, you'll become her legal owner, but she's a rare breed—very strong, very beautiful. Registration could cost you as much as a new house, and you'll accept her medical bill besides. I know you want to help, but can you really afford this girl?"

Ken chuckled to himself. "As it turns out, I've been saving up for a new house," he said, gazing tenderly across the mod's pale, peaceful, sleeping face. "But I think I'd rather give her a new home."

CHAPTER TWO

"You're not my pet."

Ken bought the stray mod, who didn't even need a name on the registration form, and within minutes, U-GeneTech assigned her a number, issued him an ownership licence, and handed him a bag of medical supplies. Evidently the hospital released mods even if they couldn't walk under their own power, because before the sun rose that morning, an intern delivered the woman to his apartment. She sat slumped in a wheelchair, sedated in a paper gown, like an oven on a dolly.

"Where do you want her?" the intern asked, as if she was a piece of furniture, an object.

Too appalled to speak, Ken hoisted the mod out of her chair, carried her into his living room, and then laid her carefully on one of his couches. She murmured softly, eyes and tongue lolling.

"Enjoy," the intern said on his way out.

Ken slammed and locked the door.

"Forget him," he told the woozy woman. "Forget your last owner. If you ever can, forget that whole nightmare. It's over now. You're safe..."

She fell asleep while he spoke. Ken brushed her bangs away from her eyes, adjusted her until she lay comfortably, and pulled his second sofa to the front door. He sat heavily, blocking her escape, intending to wait for her to wake, but the moment he relaxed, fatigue ground him into the cushions.

"I'll be right here," he mumbled, too exhausted to change out of his work clothes. "I'm sure you'll be confused and scared, waking up next to a stranger, but please...don't kill me...in my sleep..."

Ken dreamed of riots.

He dreamed of bullets piercing hordes of protesters. He dreamed of flaming bottles bursting against plastic shields. He dreamed of monsters, enormous mods bred for war, rippling with muscle, ripping rebels apart—

He awoke to silence, peace, sunlight, and an empty home.

Shooting upright, heart thumping, Ken rushed to the other couch, as if the mod had somehow turned invisible, and touching her broke the spell. *Shit,* he thought. *I blocked the front door, but...*

He sprinted to his bedroom, checking the fire escape. The window was locked from the inside. *She's still here, huh? But where?* Ken scoured his apartment, looking beneath his bed, peeking into the bathtub, searching in cupboards, but the woman seemingly vanished. He returned to the living room, baffled, and then he spotted it—a fluffy black tail poking out from the curtains.

...Seriously?

"All right, come on out," he said, waiting with his hand on his hip. She pretended not to hear. "I can see you, you know."

Cautiously as disarming a bomb, she grabbed her tail and tucked it behind the curtain.

Ken exhaled, scratching his head.

"Come on," he said, approaching her pathetic hiding place. He heard her breathing quicken. "There's nothing to be afraid of anymore."

He slowly peeled back the curtain, seeing her in the sun for the first time. About six feet tall, she timidly gazed down at him through her bangs with icy blue eyes, clutching her skimpy hospital gown to the soft, lascivious curves of her hard, slender body. Fur helped hide the scars around her throat, but her short, scruffy hair couldn't even conceal her pointed ears, much less wrap her neck.

"Hey, girl... I'm Ken," he said awkwardly. "I'm, uh... your new owner, I guess."

Gradually, her timid gaze turned ferocious. She snarled, but Ken ignored her warning.

"Relax," he said, reaching up to pet her head. "You're not really afraid of me, are you?"

He lightly touched her hair—and she attacked.

Ken reflexively raised his hands in defence, but she bit deep into his arm and forced him to the floor, thrashing her head and sawing through his flesh. He screamed as her teeth grated his bones and his blood squirted inside her mouth, and he raised his free hand, balling it up into a fist, but she suddenly stopped chewing. Leaving her teeth in him, she glared straight through his pupils.

"*Do it!*" Ken could almost hear her thinking. "*Hit me, and I'll tear off your arm!*"

Through her jaws, he felt the power vibrating within her body. She could kill him whenever she liked, he realized. If he threw a single punch, she'd probably catch his fist with one hand, grab his throat with the other, and rip out every pipe and vein. For one terrifying second, he understood why her previous owner shocked and shackled her, but that was exactly why he could never strike her.

Lowering his fist, he felt her bite loosen. Every trembling part of him wanted to yank his arm free and flee, except for the one part that knew with absolute clarity what to say next.

"S-See?" he began, summoning every ounce of willpower he could to sound calm. "You see? You're not afraid of me at all."

Something softened in her eyes, but she didn't let him go, so he kept talking.

"Whoever hurt you...I'm sorry. I'm sorry for everything you went through at your old home, and on the streets, and...I'm sorry, but I promise, I won't let anyone hurt you ever again!"

Ken felt tears sting his eyes, but she didn't let him go, so he kept talking.

"I'll protect you. I'll help you. I'll cook for you and hold you and give you whatever you need, so please... Please, just let me... Just let me make you happy, *dumbass*!"

Surprised by his outburst, the mod released her bite and crawled off Ken. He winced, as sticky strings of blood and saliva chased her black lips backward. She sat on her feet for a minute, staring remorsefully at his mauled arm, then she leaned forward—and licked his open wounds.

Charmed and disgusted, he watched her long tongue lap up his blood, letting her apologize in her own weird way. Somehow her awkward cleaning barely hurt, even when she dipped her slippery tongue into the frayed holes, and when she removed her head he noticed the bleeding had stopped, and his wound tingled.

Mouth a crimson mess, she stared at the carpet, embarrassed. Then she bowed, waiting. Ken blushed when he understood what she wanted. Tentatively, he stretched out his good arm. Her ears twitched at his touch, and all her muscles cramped up at once, but when he stroked her scruffy head, she melted, as though his petting compared to an oily massage. He might have heard her moan.

"It's all right," he said. "I shouldn't have tried to touch you like that. It's my fault, too."

He stopped rubbing her head, and she pouted, gazing longingly after his hand.

"Does it really feel that good?" Ken asked, but when he reached out to her again, she slapped his hand, jumped to her feet, stomped into the bathroom, and slammed the door. He couldn't know for certain with all the blood on her face, but he thought he saw her cheeks glowing.

As she showered, Ken remembered he stored his disinfectant and bandages in the bathroom. Rather than wait for her finish, or risk his life breaking in, he dug into the bag of medical supplies the hospital gave him and retrieved a tube labeled Re-GeneGro. At the kitchen sink he cleaned his wound, but after washing out her tingly saliva, blood spewed from the unclogged pits. He squeezed the tube, slathering his forearm with bright blue gunk—"*Graahk!*"

Ken collapsed, gurgling in agony, gripping his rigid, twitching arm. It hurt worse than the bite. Much worse. Red and white foam bubbled from his wound, blending into a pink froth that scorched his skin. His fingers curled up like a dead tarantula, his veins wriggled, and he may have passed out, because the next thing he knew the foam had dissolved. Pallid pink blobs of squishy flesh now filled the once frayed teeth marks, like potholes stuffed with sand.

"I'll never use this stuff on her," he croaked, grabbing the counter and pulling himself up.

He rinsed off the residue and patted his forearm dry with a cloth. According to the tube, his new flesh would stiffen within a few hours, at which time it would assume his skin tone. No physical evidence would remain. Just as he wondered how well the mod's leg had healed, she emerged from the washroom wearing nothing but a towel.

Out of courtesy and curiosity, he looked down at her leg. Fuzzy patches cut through the longer fur, like fast greens on a wooded golf course, but aside from some missing hair she showed no signs of assault. Inevitably Ken's eyes wandered upward. He gulped. Her towel barely clung to her perky breasts, and her once scruffy hair hung in smooth black icicles. Once she had his attention, she bared her teeth, raised her fist to her mouth, and shook her hand side to side.

"Um...?" Ken interpreted her dance. "You want a toothbrush?"

She nodded.

"Oh... I don't think I have any new ones. Just use mine for now, if you're okay with that."

She sighed and shut herself back inside the bathroom. Ken tossed the Re-GeneGro tube back into the hospital bag and moved into his bedroom to pick something to wear. Red speckles dyed his work clothes, and a nurse had thrown his bloodstained jacket into a biological waste bin last night. Fortunately his closet contained spare work outfits. Unfortunately it contained nothing fitting for a beautiful woman.

She managed to find something to suit her anyway. After Ken brushed his teeth with a brush that tasted like blood and washed in a shower that smelled like blood, he found her lounging on the couch in his clothes. Barefoot, she wore a sleeveless denim jacket with nothing underneath, zipped just high enough to hide her nipples, and a pair of racy denim shorts he couldn't recall buying.

"Hey," Ken said, tying his tiny ponytail and straightening his chef's uniform. "*Hey*," he added irritably, when he noticed the shredded denim strewn across the room. "Did you rip my clothes?"

She shrugged, gazing at the ceiling.

"We'll go shopping on one of my days off, okay? Don't just destroy my stuff."

She shrugged again.

"And why are you laying on *that* couch? I have to leave for work."

She shrugged once more, stretching out on the sofa that still blocked the door.

He murmured inaudibly, "Stupid dog..."

She flipped him the middle finger—

"*Gyuh!*" He reacted as though she stabbed him, shocked by her sense of hearing.

She flipped him the other one.

"Whatever," he grumbled. "I won't be back for a while, so help yourself to the fridge. There's nothing in there but raw ingredients...but I'll cook you something nice tonight, to celebrate our first day together. Of course, you might not even be here tonight," he said, sounding somewhat lonesome. "Honestly, you could leave today if you want."

Startled, she swivelled his way.

"I mean it," said Ken. "You're not my pet. You're free, so you can leave whenever you want. Just know that you'll always have a home here, and I'll do whatever I can for you. Sound good?"

He smiled disarmingly. She gawked at him, tilting her head and twisting her mouth.

"*Hmph,*" she snorted, leaping from one couch to the other.

"Anyway," Ken said, tugging the vacated couch away from the front door, "I'll see you later, maybe. And by the way," he added, before he left, "you look really nice, all cleaned up."

She huffed and purposely ignored him, snuggling into the cushions for a nap.

Ken performed his duties at the restaurant like a defective machine, his mind elsewhere.

"Wake up, Ken!" Trish scolded him. "That's the second steak you've burned. How long are you going to make those people wait, huh? Get it together!"

He wondered if he had sounded manipulative to his mod. He told her she could leave, but at best, she could gamble on another owner at a shelter, risking hard labour and servitude. He suspected that after a life of chains and electricity, she would frolic outdoors, reveling in her newfound freedom, so he didn't expect her to sit at the door waiting for him to come home.

She defied his expectations, but not his suspicions.

Exiting the elevator to his third floor apartment with a small bag of toothbrushes, Ken found her sulking outside his door, her feet cluttered with dirt and grass. She sat seething at the doorknob.

"Locked yourself out, eh?" he nearly laughed.

She glared at him, canine teeth burrowing into her lower lip.

"Go wash up," he said, unlocking and opening the door. "I'll fix dinner while you're in the tub."

As she showered, Ken gaped at the open refrigerator, twitching. She had eaten all the bags of vegetables. She had eaten all the blocks of cheese. She had even eaten all the raw meat, but he refused to cook the frozen or dehydrated meals in his freezer or pantry. He had promised her a celebratory dinner, so he literally ran to the supermarket, acquired ingredients for a simple stir-fry, and returned before she finished washing her feet.

As he fried the beef, peppers, and noodles, she burst from the bathroom and eagerly sniffed over the stove, content to stick her head into the sizzling wok. She grinned goofily, adding trickles of drool to the sweet and sour sauce.

"Get out of there!" Ken shoved her face. She snapped at his fingers, and he rapped her with his spoon. "And put on some clothes!"

She waddled away, clutching her wet towel to her chest. Water dripped off her luxurious tail. He snuck a peek at her shapely ass, but she snarled at him and scratched for his eyes.

"Put on some clothes, then!" he roared, whacking her again with his spoon. She growled but eventually left to pull on the denim outfit she had dropped on the bathroom floor, taking some time to wash the sauce from his spoon out of her hair.

Ken served her at the kitchen table while the meal still steamed. She panted with excitement, tensely gripping her fork and knife.

"To you and me, I guess," Ken said, scraping a heavy helping onto her plate.

For a few minutes, she maintained the patience to skewer her food before shovelling it into her mouth, but soon she sunk her nails into the flavourful pile, chomping at handfuls of crispy bits. She then snatched Ken's meal away from him, tilting the contents down her convulsing throat.

"Stupid dog," Ken said, utensils trembling in his hands.

She flipped him the finger, licking his plate clean.

Ken couldn't stock fresh foods without her promptly emptying his fridge, so he bought only what they needed for their next meal, including whole meals from work. Over the next week she slept most of the time, dodging Ken except during dinner, but if his food made her smile each night, he went to bed happy. According to the muddy footprints in their apartment, she ran through fields to break up her boredom, but once she could relax around Ken, she constantly teased him for fun.

Ken was convinced she hurriedly set up pranks whenever she smelled him coming. In truth, when she wasn't exploring the more verdant corners of the city, she spent most of her time dreaming up fun new ways to torment him. One day she awaited him after work on a throne of mangled pillows, with stuffing wedged in her teeth. One evening she posed provocatively on the edge of his peripheral vision, slapping him across the face every time he looked. One night she even joined him in bed, but she conveniently stretched in her sleep to kick him tumbling off the mattress.

But she especially enjoyed customizing his clothes with her claws.

She always trimmed off the sleeves and legs, turning T-shirts into tank tops and shorts into shorter shorts. Her fur warmed her enough already, so she exposed as much skin as possible, but Ken preferred her half-naked to fully clothed—for his own sanity. The first time she wore long pants, she writhed and whined irresistibly, rubbing her overheated thighs until he needed to leave the room.

Frustrated in more ways than one, Ken finally took her shopping.

He donned a casual dinner jacket, as if anticipating a romantic outing with her, and then they rode a private pod to the biggest, busiest mall in the city. Bristling at the pod's high speeds, she leaned across Ken's lap, beating her tail against one window while peering happily out the other, but when they arrived at the mall, the claustrophobic crowds, echoing music, and lurid lights overwhelmed her senses. She regressed into a puppy, hiding behind Ken and nuzzling his spine, but when he held her hand, caressing the squishy pink pads on her palms, she walked along calmly—or at least calmer.

She buried her face into Ken when they passed adults, especially men, but she gazed curiously after kids, who pointed at her and giggled to their parents. Ken noticed the dirty looks strangers shot at him, but other mod owners greeted him in passing, as if to say, "You get it. You're one of us."

He hated that more than the dirty looks.

The other owners tied their pets with leashes and shock collars, prepared to forcibly control or punish them the moment they disobeyed. As slaves who learned obedience through pain, the mods with shock collars appeared depressed and frightened, though many of the leashed mods cheerfully followed their masters. Like lost children, they desired dependency, security, and guidance.

Self-conscious about the leash he'd tied around his own mod, Ken released her downy hand, but she snatched his hand right back, scowling.

"Don't be so clingy," he said. "You're not a child."

She defiantly hugged his arm so tight she pressed it between her breasts through her shirt. Her fuzzy cushions enveloped his elbow in heat. Ken pouted at her, embarrassed, but she just stuck out her tongue and knowingly winked. He averted his face so she wouldn't see him blush.

"Whatever," he said coolly. "But you're holding my hand, not the other way around."

She held his hand, not the other way around, the rest of the way to the fashion boutique.

The shop sold all manner of mod apparel, such as pants with slots for tails, shoes with extra room for claws, and sturdy gear for working and hunting. It even included a section for accessories like leashes, collars, and jewelry.

Ken mostly avoided that section, leading her toward more freeing clothing.

They browsed the boutique, amassing piles of clothes for her to model later. She occasionally yanked something off the racks, eyes twinkling, but mainly he suggested items for her, and she shook her head or nodded. She refused to wear a bra, as it added undesirable warmth, but she liked skirts because her legs stayed cool. She liked lacy panties and open-toed shoes for similar reasons, and she sought tops that exposed her midriff, the coolest spot on her body with the least amount of hair.

Ken lost track of time watching her twirl and strut in different colours and combinations, as they chose which clothes to buy. Hours into their shopping session, he found his personal favourite.

"This one's cute," he claimed, presenting the faded black leather vest. "I found it in the hunting section. I mean, it's got sheaths for knives stitched on the inside... but it's kind of pretty, right?"

She grimaced, instantly dismissing the hot, heavy garment.

"Come on, give it chance. It has no sleeves," he pitched. "It's got buttons, so you don't have to wear an undershirt or worry about zippers getting caught in your hair. It's short, too, so it'll show off your stomach. And look." He displayed the collar, a black and white puff. "It matches your fur."

He dumped it on her shoulders. She fussed like a toddler, as he shoved her arms through the holes, but once Ken pushed her into the vest, she paused in wonder at her reflection in the mirror. The puffy collar blended into her complexion, partially obscuring her scarred neck. She stroked her throat, as if grasping a memory, and then she posed dramatically, peeking over the collar, buttoning and unbuttoning the front. Finally she laughed, quick and sharp as a bark, yet sweet and smooth as honey, like the chime of a bell.

Ken smiled at the sound. "See? I knew you'd like it. Think we've got enough clothes now?"

She nodded once, beaming.

"Hm..." He hesitated. "I don't know. I still feel like you're missing something."

She tilted her head, puzzled.

"Never mind. I'm sure I'll remember later. I'll just pay for these, then we'll head out, okay?"

As the sun sank into the red summer sky, they arrived home. They tumbled through the door onto the floor, encumbered in shopping bags. She sprawled on top of Ken, taking a moment to fix her skirt, and then she squeezed him and purred appreciatively.

"Y-Yeah, you're welcome," he said, patting her head. "But hold up; I got something for you."

She clumsily rolled over, letting him stand. He shut the door and flicked on the lights, then he searched through the shopping bags, digging near the bottoms until he pulled out what looked like a massive wristwatch. She crouched, squinting up at him, as he tucked her present behind his back.

"Did you know my parents were slaves?" he asked, taking her aback. "They died before I can remember, but a lot of people have stories like mine. Do you want to hear it?"

The woman nodded. Ken took a deep breath and began.

"Well, when all the slaves were freed, a lot of them had kids, thinking they would finally get jobs and be able to start families. Except that never happened. The government wanted to avoid war, so they just replaced human slaves with mods. Other nations didn't think of mods as people, so they allowed it. The threat of a war was over, but just like that, thousands of people were homeless and unemployed. There was an uprising, but the Free Slaves lost...and suddenly I was alone.

"I drifted from crappy foster home, to crappy orphanage, to foster home, but wherever I went, people beat me and used me until I just wanted to die. Imagine, a little boy wanting to kill himself..."

He stopped, staring into the ground. The woman carefully approached.

"But then I met my sister, Trish," he said tenderly. "I'll never know why she cared so much. Maybe she just wanted someone to live for, but she saved me, and I finally found happiness because she gave me the love and support I needed. And that's the kind of person I want to be for you."

By then she had embraced him, caressing his neck with her fuzzy cheek. She stroked his hair, brushing his little ponytail loose. His dark locks unfurled, and silky shadow-tips tickled her face.

"I wasn't sure at first, but now I know," said Ken. "From now on, it's you and me."

They detached briefly, as he removed her gift from behind his back and flattened the leather strap over his palms. The scarlet sun flickered off the golden plate, illuminating one engraved word:

Yumi.

"You and me," he said, "Yumi."

She joyously accepted her new name, hugging Ken and spinning him round. Yumi giggled, flooding their home with sharp sweet chimes, before letting him down and displaying her bare neck. He fastened the belt around it so the nameplate gleamed against her throat. Combined with the fluffy collar on her vest, the thick leather strap completely concealed the scars from her past.

CHAPTER THREE

"Run, Yumi! Run!"

From then on, Yumi never removed the vest or collar Ken had bought her except to bathe or shower. She even slept in them, preferring the supple leather to the extra fur that blankets provided. On cooler days she unbuttoned her vest and wore cute tops from the boutique underneath, but she otherwise always looked the same above the waist.

Her lower body always varied, however; today she donned a tight leather miniskirt to match her upper half, partially exposing her underpants to Ken as she rested face down on the couch, legs stretched across his lap. Ken sat watching television, playing with the bottoms of her feet. Her bumpy pink pads felt like packs of warm gel to his fingertips. During commercial breaks he massaged them, pleased by her soft squeaks of pleasure.

Suddenly Yumi kicked off the couch, jumped to the sunny window, and growled. She pressed her hands and forehead to the glass, then she barked, and barked, and barked (cutely)—"*RAWRF!*"

"Yumi?" He joined her at the window, concerned. "What's wrong? What's out there?"

Ken squinted through glaring sunlight, scanning the yard and street below. Pods zipped past on their tracks, and an older married couple he recognized from down the hall embarked on a stroll, but he couldn't spot anything alarming. On a whim he cracked open the window, and just then, on the edge of hearing, he picked up the distant yet distinct sound of rapid gunfire. He exhaled, relieved.

"Is that what you heard?" he asked, patting her head. "That's nothing. Since the slave uprising, only the police can own guns. Well, them and the military..."

Yumi glanced up at him skeptically.

"There's an academy just down the road from here," Ken explained. "The police like to train out in public to show off their power or whatever. If we're lucky, the MK9s might be practicing, too. Wanna go see?"

Ken and Yumi walked hand-in-hand toward the gunshots. She vigilantly prowled beside him, flexing her fingers into hooked blades, swivelling and sniffing in all directions.

"Would you relax?" he said. "It's fine, I'll show you—"

BANG! Another shot fired and she flailed, hopping up onto Ken. Yumi laid her trembling chin on his shoulder and squeezed him, squishing her breasts against his back. He sighed, hooked his arms under her legs, and reluctantly hauled her the rest of the way. Despite her height, she was surprisingly light, yet his legs and cheeks burned by the end of their trek.

A throng of hushed spectators had gathered by the time they arrived at the academy. Topped with razor wire, a tall wall of bulletproof plastic surrounded the grounds, allowing citizens to safely watch the police train. City officials claimed the public practices reassured citizens of their security, but Ken believed they discouraged slaves and their sympathizers from staging future rebellions.

Still, they served as decent entertainment.

"See?" Ken told Yumi, pointing to the far side of the yard. "They're just training."

Rows of recruits fired at moving paper targets, sinking bullets into hay bales if they missed, and after each round, a supervisor collected the targets to tally their scores. Yumi flinched at every gunshot, tucking her ears against her skull, but she stared unblinkingly at the mods that had drawn the awestruck crowd.

Seven feet tall, with pointed, wolfish faces and navy shorts, they lumbered on their knuckles like shaggy gorillas, strong and shockingly fast. Ken and Yumi watched one sprint a hundred yards in eight seconds and tackle another mod. The mods wrestled ferociously, tearing out clumps of grass as they rumbled in a snarling ball, until one lifted the other and dropped him headfirst into the dirt. Seemingly unfazed, the defeated mod scrambled upright, shook the victor's hand, and then the two engaged in another skirmish.

Ken glanced nervously up the bulletproof wall at the razor wire. The mods seemed powerful enough to leap over it and rampage wherever and whoever they liked, but the police had fitted their bulky necks with sleek black and yellow shock collars. For every mod wrestling and running outside, an officer patrolled close by. The officers held small devices, hovering their thumbs over the triggers that would thrust lightning bolts down the mods' throats.

Elsewhere, mods drilled by disarming knives. Police donned bite-proof armour and helmets, and they brandished short rods coursing with blue electricity. The mods deftly circled them, barely dodging stabs and swipes, and immobilized the officers. Most reached around the mock knives with their long arms, gripped the officers' wrists, and delivered a purposely weak blow, before restarting the drill. Others adopted an aggressive style, biting the officers' arms or crushing their fingers until they dropped their rods. One, however, repeatedly suffered electrical shocks, more daft than deft.

Enraged, he bulled toward his officer and threw huge, looping punches. She danced around him like a graceful matador, dragging the blue blade across his legs or poking him in the back as he passed. He rushed her again, grasping for her with open hands. She struck his outstretched palm—*ZAP!* A flurry of sparks burst against his skin, but he endured the pain and closed his fist around her rod. Her eyes expanded, as the mod effortlessly bent and broke her weapon.

"Now! Shock him *now!*" she cried, but his mighty roar drowned out her voice, and he *punched* her with his full strength. She blocked his uppercut, but Ken heard her arms *crunch*. She soared in an arc, screaming, and landed in a shattered heap. Gasps erupted through the crowd, as the mod howled in agony and convulsed grotesquely on the grass. His howls transformed into terrified gurgles, as he helplessly clutched his collar with twitching fingers. The police swiftly surrounded him and shot him full of tranquilizer darts, and they kept lethal bullets aimed at him until he passed out.

Ken suspected the mod would never regain consciousness. He smelled burning fur and flesh, and if he could smell it, the stench must have been doubly unbearable for Yumi. She quivered on his back, snuffling his hair to mask the unpleasant scents. As something wet dripped onto his scalp, he realized she was quietly crying. Her ears had amplified the policewoman's breaking bones and shrill screams, and her eyes had likely snapped shut the moment the mod started convulsing. The anguish of shock collars still scarred her skin and mind. She didn't need another painful reminder.

"I shouldn't have brought you here," Ken said, adjusting his grip on Yumi. "I'm sorry, puppy... Let's go home."

She still sniffled as he carried her into the apartment. Ken eased her off his aching back. She shuffled toward the washroom, hiding her face, but he gently grabbed her arm and spun her into his embrace. Yumi wept and shivered, clutching his head to her chest. Her sobs shook him profoundly, and tears blurred his vision, but he didn't dare let them fall. For her, he wanted to be strong.

"I'm sorry you had to see that," said Ken. "After everything you've been through, that couldn't have been easy to watch. But that's not going to happen to you, okay? You'll never be a slave again," he reassured her. They separated, and he tapped her golden nameplate. "The only collars you'll ever wear are necklaces like *these*. So don't be afraid. And don't cry anymore. I hate hearing you cry..."

Yumi nodded and relaxed. Ken sat with her on the couch, pulled a tissue from the box on the coffee table, and patted her puffy red eyes. He wiped her small dark nose. She giggled at his awkward action, then he moved to the kitchen to toss the tissues. Yumi followed him up. He dropped the tissues into the trashcan under the sink, but before he could turn around, two furry arms wrapped his waist.

Pinning him against the counter, Yumi caressed his chest and abdomen, exploring the subtle bumps and curves of his muscles. Ken gulped, and she slowly inhaled his scent. Delicately, she licked his cheek once, then twice, then again, dragging her hot wet tongue from his chin to his temple. Her tongue lingered against his skin, tasting him. Her breath brushed his lips. She punctuated her sloppy kiss with a quick *peck*—and then she bolted. Ken spun, glimpsing her red face just before she shut herself in the bathroom. He touched the tingling streak she left on his cheek.

Why are you the one embarrassed? Ken thought, feeling feverish. *Honestly...*

Ken had just inserted his homemade macaroni and cheese in the oven when Yumi returned. She fidgeted coyly, avoiding eye contact.

"I, er...work later," he said, closing the oven. "I'm just making us something quick before I go. Hope mac and cheese is all right."

She shrugged, smoothing the hair over her forearms.

"I've been wondering," Ken said, subconsciously scratching his cheek. "How old are you?"

Yumi studied her hands for a moment, then threw up two peace signs. In other words, four fingers. Ken gawked at her, recalling the eighteen-year-old child and the miracles of genetic modification—

"You're only four years old!?"

Yumi walked up to Ken, smacked him upside the head, and flashed the peace signs again.

Two twos.

"Oh," he exhaled. "You're twenty-two. About my age, then... That makes more sense."

She nodded, rolled her eyes, and dumped herself over the living room couch. From the kitchen table, Ken picked up the pad and pen he used to write grocery lists and met her on the sofa.

"Um, it's probably a little late to ask this, but," he swallowed, "what's your name?"

She looked at him, as though he'd gone insane.

"Could you maybe write it down?"

Without sitting up, Yumi stared blankly at the pad and pen.

"Do you know how to write?"

She shook her head.

"Not a word?"

She shook her head firmly.

"Oh..." he said, disappointed. "Then I guess I'll never know your real name, huh?"

She suddenly grabbed the writing utensils from him and threw them across the room. Then she gripped his collar, pulled him on top of her, and tapped a fingernail against her golden nameplate, burrowing into his heart with a stern stare.

"*This is my real name now,*" her eyes told Ken. "*You and me... Right?*"

Yumi yanked him closer, then she forcefully kissed Ken.

He resisted at first, questioning his morality, but she eased his irresolute mind by sliding her tongue into his mouth. Lust seized him, and he twisted his tongue around hers, and they embraced there, passionately suffocating each other. They came up for air, panting. He petted her head, and she squirmed beneath him, wagging her tail between their entwined legs. She licked his face, slathering him with saliva, and rubbed his hardening crotch with her thigh. Ken slipped his hand under her vest. His fingers combed through her lustrous fur, crawled over her fuzzy breast, and found the fleshy nub at the centre. He pinched gently at first, then firmly.

Yumi squeaked in pain and pleasure. She bit into his shoulder, neck, and lip, growling seductively, and then—

Beep! Beep! The fire alarm shrieked. Smoke reached their noses. *Beep! Beep!*

The exhilarating haze that clouded their judgement wafted away. Yumi groaned, reluctantly entangling herself from Ken, who rushed to extinguish the small fire. The cheese on the border of his casserole bubbled like black tar, but once he scraped the smoky crust off, the meal looked delicious, or at least edible.

Ken and Yumi ate lunch in awkward silence, as she sent him knowing smirks across the table. She later knocked at the locked bathroom door while he showered, apparently hoping he opened up, then she attempted to see him naked, blatantly barging into his bedroom while he changed. Seeking his attention, she even walked with him to work, despite his protests.

"Go home, Yumi," Ken said, as they neared the restaurant. She stubbornly tagged along. "They don't let mods inside without their owners, and I don't want my sister to know about you yet. Do you know how many knives there are in that place? If Trish finds out I bought a *slave*, she'd—"

Yumi stopped walking. Ken glanced over his shoulder, and she scowled at him, lips pursed.

"Look, you know what I meant," he said. "You're not a slave *anymore*, but...she won't get that. She'll think I bought you for...you know, and with how close we've been getting lately, I just...I don't want her to get the wrong idea about us. You understand, right?"

Yumi nodded, sulking at the sidewalk.

"I'm sorry," Ken said sincerely. "Listen... I'll try and think of a way to break it to her tonight. Come by the restaurant later, and I'll..." He breathed deeply. "I'll introduce you two. Sound good?"

She nodded again, simpering slightly.

"Good... Now, before you head back, do you have your key on you?"

She rolled her eyes and patted her vest pocket.

"Just checking. Have fun without me, I guess. I'll see you soon, all right?"

Yumi jogged up to him, quickly licked his cheek, and then started home. As he walked alone, Ken contemplated their relationship. Their rapid progress should have thrilled him, yet an uneasy emotion swirled within his belly, something wavering between insecurity, suspicion, and anxiety.

"Do mods ever go into heat?" Ken asked Trish, mere minutes into his shift. He stuck a rack of pre-boiled ribs on the barbeque. "You know, like dogs?"

"Do they *what?*" She scratched her bushy orange mane. "Where the hell did that come from?"

"I was just wondering," Ken said, hardly heard over the clattering and clanking in the kitchen. He glanced sideways down the line, wary of the other cooks overhearing. "Like, if one of the servers suddenly started making out with me, it might not be because she fell in love with me, right? Maybe she was just in heat, and I just happened to be the closest guy at the time."

"What're you trying to tell me?" Trish asked, lowering her normally noisy voice. "Did you do something with one of the mods? I've told you a hundred times, Ken, those girls are off-limits!" She nudged his arm. "So, which one was it? The blonde one with the big tits? It was, wasn't it?"

"No," Ken said, saucing the sizzling ribs. "I'm just curious, that's all."

Trish sighed, exasperated. "Just keep your *furry* fantasies to yourself, all right?"

"Yeah, sure," he mumbled.

Just then, a cashier shouted from the lobby: "Ma'am? You can't go back there! Down, girl!"

A black and white, leather clad beauty busted through the swinging kitchen door.

"Yu—!?" Ken slapped his hand over his mouth.

"You...?" Trish blinked at the mystery mod. "Ken, do you know this girl?"

Flustered by her abrupt appearance, Ken considered shooing Yumi out of the restaurant, but when he saw the fear and tears on her face, he dashed forward and hugged her, drawing every eye in the kitchen. Trish gaped at them dumbfounded, her jaw ajar.

Ken separated from Yumi and clasped her quivering hands. She panted from sprinting.

"Are you okay?" he asked. "What happened out there?"

Suddenly a long, lonely howl shook the restaurant, like a great horn blasting off the bow of a ship. Yumi dragged Ken toward the rear fire exit. Trish's voice chased them, but he couldn't hear her with that howl echoing against his eardrums.

As they barged through the backdoor and out into the orange evening sun, Ken asked Yumi, "What's happening? What about my sister?"

Yumi ignored him in her panic, strengthened her hold on his wrist, and leaped down the stairs leading from the backdoor, forcing him to follow. She pulled him through the parking lot, and as they rounded the restaurant, Ken peered inside through the front windows, and the fear that gripped Yumi sunk its talons deep into his brain.

Smashing benches and bones, a bulky brown monster rampaged in the lobby, fighting toward the kitchen. A few mods valiantly defended the many humans, but the brute stood almost ten feet tall, dwarfing even the MK9s on the police force. The servers stood no chance. It lifted the frilly waitresses and hurled them against the walls, swinging waiters by their ties and tails clear across the room.

"Is that a war mod?" Ken said, trembling. "What the hell is a *bloodhound* doing here?"

He could easily imagine the hound charging at frontlines in impenetrable armour, although it wore nothing today, as if it had outgrown all available clothing. Its head, with its almost cute, floppy ears, looked two sizes too small, but its muscles seemed so stuffed with meat they might split.

Ken watched in horror as Trish approached the monster with a fire extinguisher.

"*Idiot!*" he shouted. He dug his shoes into the concrete, and he and Yumi skidded to a stop. "What the hell is she thinking?"

Trish sprayed the beast with white smoke. On her signal, some servers who cowered behind the front desk snuck around the blinded beast, escaping and scattering outside. Customers and cooks flooded the parking lot, exiting via the kitchen and then speeding off in their cars, but the hound had cornered Trish. It stomped toward her, wiping foam off its face, as her extinguisher sputtered out.

Suddenly a blond boy chomped into the hound's arm, allowing Trish to flee into the kitchen. Max's teeth sliced through its tough skin, but it clutched his head, peeled him off like a loose sticker, and chucked him through the front window—*CRASH!*

Max lay bloody and limp in the parking lot on a bed of shattered glass. Cars narrowly missed crushing him as they fled, and people on foot sprinted over and around his body. Ken wanted to run as desperately as any of them, but he couldn't find Trish in the frenzied crowd, and fear froze his feet. For some reason, the beast locked eyes with him, then with Yumi. It hopped through the jagged hole in the broken window.

Then, it charged.

It knocked a moving car out of its path like a pebble, and while Ken struggled to comprehend its size and power, it bowled him over and scooped up Yumi, wrapping her waist with one huge hand. The hound jogged away with her, quaking the ground with each heavy step, but she twisted in its grip and kicked its wrinkled face. Its nose *cracked* under her toes, and it dropped her and roared, rattling the glass shards on the cement, but before Yumi could return to Ken, the hound caught her tail and hoisted her up. She flailed like a fish on a hook, scratching for its eyes, but it dangled her out of reach, so she jammed her claws into the bleeding holes Max had chewed into its arm. It roared again, but rather than drop her, it squeezed her tail and grasped for her like a ripe apple hanging from a branch. Yumi swung by her tail and dodged its hand by millimeters, but as she swung back like a pendulum, the beast clutched her head and smothered her inside its palm. She fought for breath, raking her nails across its hand and tearing out strips of skin until her fingers were red and slippery. It grimaced and growled, but it didn't let go. Her lungs shuddered in agony. Clawing at life, she gradually wilted—

"*GWAARGH!*" the monster screeched.

Yumi fell to the concrete, waking with a gasp. Cotton clogged her ringing brain, and her tail and torso throbbed, but her keen senses speared through the pain and sunlight to make out a murky silhouette perched upon the war mod. The shadow tugged a massive kitchen knife out of the hound's shoulder, then plunged the blade into its back and neck, punctuating each vicious stab with a word: "Let—her—go—you—freak!"

Someone helped her up, then inexplicably shoved her on her back. Her cloudy vision cleared, revealing a tall ginger woman.

"Go, kid!" said Trish. "It chased you here; it's after *you*!"

"Run, Yumi!" Ken cried from above. "Run!"

Yumi frantically rolled over and then bounded away on all fours. She hopped the hood of a pickup truck, raced past a sprinting couple as if they were jogging, and darted into a maze of alleys. Tears stung her eyes as she abandoned Ken, but she obeyed his command and ran, and ran, and ran.

Meanwhile Ken rode the colossus like a bucking bull, clinging to clumps of fur. It thrashed and screamed beneath him, unable to reach him with its chunky, cumbersome arms, yet he was slipping. Blood spewed from the slits Ken had carved into its muscles, drenching his hands, and he slid off its slick back, dragging his knife through its flesh on his way down.

He urgently crawled away, expecting the beast to grab his head, pluck him off the ground, and squeeze his skull until it popped like an egg, but astonishingly, it ignored Ken. It shot him a disgusted look over its leaking shoulder, but then it immediately ran toward the alley where Yumi vanished.

"Hey!" Ken shouted, standing up and brandishing his blade. "Your fight's with me! *Hey!*"

"Forget that girl," Trish said, jogging to his side. "She's gone."

"I won't give up on her! Let's just hijack one of these cars and—"

"No, I mean she's gone, as in she got away, as in she's safe." Trish pointed at the beast. "*Look.*"

The hound sniffed the air and sidewalk, then wiped its nose. It repeated this twice, rubbing its face more aggressively each time, until it howled in frustration. Because he had attacked it from behind, Ken hadn't noticed at first, but blood poured from the creature's nostrils.

"I saw that girl break his nose while you were on the ground," said Trish. "I'm not an expert, but if it can't track her scent, I doubt it'll find her."

"I see..." Ken said, relatively reassured. "Thanks for the knife, by the way."

"I didn't bring it for you; you just took it. Anyway, we need to leave." Trish grabbed his arm like that of a misbehaving child. She pulled him through the parking lot, weaving between hurried, honking drivers that had jammed themselves into gridlock. "War mods can absorb bullets. It might look like you did some damage with that knife, but their skin is a foot deep in parts, like *meat armour.* If that thing sets its sights on us, we're fuc—"

"*RWAAUGH!*" a vengeful roar erupted behind them.

They heard metal and glass crunching, and when they looked back, the beast was charging at them like a tank through the congested parking lot, flipping and flattening cars.

"Go!" Trish yelled at Ken, pushing him left and running right. A truck spun through the air and crashed between them. "Go, GO!"

Ken raced toward the sidewalk, hopping a speed bump and then hurdling a shrub. His heart pounded his ribs, his shoes clapped the concrete, and his arms pumped at his sides so fast he nearly stabbed himself with his knife. He glanced over his shoulder to check on Trish, hoping and fearing it had followed her instead, but it galloped straight for him, gaining with every ungainly stride. Pushing his physical limits, he ran so hard his knees nearly buckled from the shock, yet still he heard heated panting, and he thought he felt giant fingers graze the back of his jacket. If he kept to the sidewalk, the beast would surely catch and kill him—so he recklessly ran into rush hour traffic.

A pod *whooshed* past him so close the wind nearly knocked the knife from his hand, and a car braked with a *screech* to avoid clipping Ken. All around him, tires squealed and horns honked. Every step brought a brush with death, but if he hesitated, the war mod would rip him apart, so he stared dead ahead and sprinted toward the other side of the street.

A pod approached, rounding the curve. It launched at Ken like a missile, but when it entered his peripheral vision, he reflexively dove, rolling to the sidewalk, as it almost smashed his ankle. Only then did he dare look back. The beast glared at him, still standing on the opposite curb.

"Hah!" Ken taunted it, surging with adrenaline. "What's wrong? Too scared to... *Shit!*"

The hound stepped backward, then charged forward and jumped, soaring across six lanes of traffic. Shading Ken, it eclipsed the sun, then landed beside him—*BOOM!*—cracking the cement.

The quake unbalanced Ken, but he bravely attacked the mod before it could recover from the drop. He stabbed at its bowed head, but it raised its hand, and he plunged the blade into its palm instead. It snapped its hand shut like a giant clam to crush Ken's arms, but he hastily leaped back, tripping to the sidewalk. Casually picking the knife out of its skin like a splinter, the beast stomped toward Ken. He crawled away like a flustered crab, but with one effortless swipe, it scooped him up off the ground. Snarling, it steadily lifted him toward its face, drawing him so close their noses nearly touched.

Ken chuckled audaciously.

"What's the matter, creep? Your date run out on you?"

The bloodhound growled, as if to say, *"It's your fault she got away. I almost had her!"*

"If you thought I'd just run away and let you take that girl, I guess you know better now, huh?" Ken said, motioning to its punctured shoulder. "I'll fight for her, even if it kills me!"

The beast grinned. *"Have it your way,"* it seemed to say, and it squeezed Ken, constricting his lungs. His ribs creaked, and his eyes bulged, and his life slowly leaked from his lips. He struggled to inhale, squeaking and rasping. The monster laughed, emitting a low, satisfied rumble like an engine revving, as blood trickled from its nostrils, painting its smile bright red. It strangled his entire body, exposing only his head to watch his anguished face shift from beige to blue. Suddenly its sadistic smile faded into a scowl. Winding up, it brought Ken behind its head, then *whipped* him like a ball.

Ken whirled through the air, disorientated, and then slammed into a hot, hairy cushion. Yumi braced her long legs, absorbing the full force of his fall without budging, and she cradled him like an infant, as he gasped and coughed in her arms. He tried to derive comfort from her normally soft body, but she felt wrong. Her heartbeat was a frightening hum, and her muscles were steel rods coated in stiff rubber. Her veins pulsed beneath her steaming skin, as if her blood was literally boiling. Her fur bristled like porcupine quills, and her breath hissed between her teeth in searing bursts.

"Yumi..." Ken exhaled, astounded. "What happened to you?"

She set him down, patted his head, and marched toward the war mod.

"Stop, Yumi! You don't have to fight. You can outrun it. Just leave me and—"

Yumi spun on Ken and paralyzed him with a furious, dogged glare. "*That's not fair,*" her eyes conveyed. "*You're allowed to die for me, but I can't risk my life for you? You've rescued me twice, Ken. Now, it's my turn to protect you!*"

"*GRAAAH!*" the war mod roared, charging Yumi. Its footsteps sent tremors through her body, but she faced it fearlessly. She crouched and shrieked, baring her teeth and claws, and for a second, Ken couldn't decide which mod terrified him more. The beast grasped at Yumi, but she shot between its open arms, pointed her feet, and speared its gut with her toenails. It doubled over and gripped her legs, groaning, but she curled her toes into barbs, and when it yanked, it ripped out chunks of its own flesh—*SPLASH!* It screamed, reeling, releasing his prey to cup both hands over the gushing chink in its armour. Yumi sprang upward so fast she blurred, smashing her knee into the hound's unguarded jaw. She rose even higher, ever *higher*, then plummeted, and as she neared the beast, she performed a graceful front flip and crashed her heel into its skull—*CRACK!*

It clutched its head, wailing. Yumi landed with a little bounce, as though her legs were springs, then she chomped into the beast's abdomen, tore out a stringy, mangled lump of meat, and spit it on the ground. She ferociously scratched at the hole, digging toward the organs inside, but the war mod captured her once more. She struggled in its grip, though not for long. Hooking a couple of its fingers under her armpits, she torqued her body—*KRIK!*—dislocating its knuckles and freeing herself. Again the hound roared, more in frustration than pain. Desperately abandoning all attempts to restrain her, it clenched its uninjured hand and swung it down on Yumi like a sledgehammer.

Yumi evaded the blow—*BOOM!*—and the cement splintered beneath her feet. Punches rained on her— *BOOM! BOOM! BOOM!*—shattering the sidewalk, but she dizzyingly dodged the hound's fists, bending her lithe body around every earthshaking bomb while weaving between its legs. It stamped its feet like a toddler on a tantrum, kicking up dust and rocks. She avoided the falling pillars, slashing through thighs and calves after each angry stomp, but then the beast abruptly ran away. Yumi relaxed at its retreat, then tensed in terror when she realized where it was headed. During the frenzied battle, they switched positions. The hound was now between her and Ken, chasing him down the sidewalk.

Lowering herself to all fours, Yumi kicked off the broken concrete and broke into a full sprint. She zipped past storefronts and streetlamps, and when she hit her top speed, she *jumped*. From forty feet up, she noticed that the hound was hobbling from its injuries, though it had nearly caught Ken. At the peak of her leap, she curled into a cannonball and dropped, and as the hound pounced at Ken, she unfurled, kicking its head like an oversized arrow and *crushing* it into the ground.

As the creature stirred on its hands and knees, Yumi bit one of its floppy ears. She gnawed on the leathery flap like a chew toy and then violently *ripped* her head sideways. The skin stretched like gum, then *snapped*. The hound howled and writhed, holding its gooey earhole, and crawled away on its back. Yumi stalked the beast. Its ear poked through her lips like a fuzzy brown tongue. She spit it out, seething, and steam hissed from her mouth. The hound scrambled upright and cowered away, waving one hand in surrender, but she rushed forward and grabbed the muscle dangling between its legs. A look of horror crossed its face, as she threateningly pressed her fingertips against its spongy shaft, drawing out red droplets. Yumi glared upward into the bloodhound's eyes, as sirens echoed in the distance. It nodded meekly. She let go, and then it fled, galloping into a nearby alley.

"Yumi!" Ken called, but she didn't react, as if she couldn't hear him. "Yumi, are you all right?" He embraced her from behind, but she didn't react, as if she couldn't feel him. "I thought I'd have to watch you die. I was so scared, but...thank you. Thank you for coming back... Are you okay?"

Finally, Yumi reacted. She spun to face him, eyes brimming with tears, and then she shook her head, hugged him, and wept. Ken squeezed her hard, overheated body. Her humming heart vibrated against his chest, as she sobbed and convulsed, but in a few minutes, after the police and paramedics arrived, her heart rate dropped. Her muscles softened. Her sobbing ceased. And she collapsed.

CHAPTER FOUR

"I guess we're an official couple now."

Ken awoke to piercing pain in his shin. Confused and angry, he swiveled in his uncomfortable chair, peering about the unfamiliar white room. Trish glowered down at him, impatiently tapping her foot, while Yumi slept beside him in a glass chamber. Vapour rose from her skin and lips, fogging the inside like a mirror after a hot shower, and water droplets trickled down the outside. Ken wiped some condensation off the cold glass to better view her peaceful face, then rubbed his stinging shin.

"Why'd you have to kick me?" Ken whined at Trish.

"As exciting as it is watching you sleep, I got sick of waiting," she said, looking at the chamber. "How's your pet girlfriend holding up?"

"She's not my pet," spat Ken.

"But she is your girlfriend?"

"I dunno," he mumbled. "She's doing better, anyway. At least, she seemed all right when she was awake earlier. With her heat stroke and the heart attack, she's really weak, but her doctor said she can come home once her fever drops below 102." He checked the monitor on the chamber that displayed her core temperature. It read 103.8. "Hm... It's gone down a few degrees, at least."

"You just sort of took off yesterday," said Trish. "Have you been here all night?"

"I went home for a bit to change and pack some stuff, but otherwise, yeah."

"But you're okay, right? Nothing's broken or anything?"

"I'm a little sore, but like I told you over the phone, and in my many, *many* texts, I'm fine."

"All right, sorry I asked. I came to check up on you, but I guess I should just leave, huh?"

"Well, you didn't have to come. You could've just called. Again."

"Whatever," Trish huffed, storming toward the door. "Do what you want, see if I care—"

"I'm kidding!" Ken called her back. "I'm glad you're worried about me. Now, would you sit?" He patted the empty chair on his left. "Please?"

Trish glanced tentatively between him and the seat, as if suspecting some horrible trap, then stomped at the chair, slammed herself into it, and folded her arms. Ken so rarely saw her outside the restaurant, he'd forgotten how cute she could look in street clothes. Long necklaces drooped into her ample cleavage, which he guiltily glanced into, before scanning the rest of her body. Her vibrant top and tight jeans accentuated her voluptuous figure. He almost asked if her pants were too hot, but then he remembered she didn't have fur.

"Just so you know, Max didn't make it," she said bluntly.

He gawked at her, incredulous. "What?"

"That war mod broke his neck, apparently, when it threw him through that window. Sorry." Trish patted his back. "I know you liked the kid."

Ken's head hung heavy in his hands, and he rubbed his drowsy eyes.

"How can you say that?" he asked the tiled floor. Trish raised an eyebrow. "He saved your life, didn't he? He worked with us for like a year. How can you talk about him like he didn't even matter? Don't you feel anything?"

"Of course I do," Trish snapped. "What? If I don't cry, that means I don't care? It's not like we were close. It's sad, but mods die. People die. Kids die. Do you just weep every time you watch the news? You can't get all depressed over every little tragedy, especially when it comes to mods."

"But he didn't just die. He was *killed* by that... monster. Damn it!" Ken whirled out of his seat, pacing across the room. "Where the hell did that thing come from, anyway?"

"According to the news, no one knows yet. Thanks to you and your girl here, it bled all over the place, but its DNA or whatever wasn't in any of U-GeneTech's records. So, it really could've come from anywhere. Maybe the Free Slaves are breeding some secret army? That's my guess, anyway."

"Where would some small underground group like the Free Slaves get hold of a *bloodhound*? That'd be like a street gang getting their hands on a tank."

"Kind of, but not really. They're insanely expensive, sure, but it's not like they're illegal to own. The rich and famous use them as bodyguards all the time."

"Still, I doubt they could afford one."

"Well, someone could be supplying them with eggs."

Ken blinked vacantly. He imagined a puppy breaking free from an eggshell and yawning.

"Mods aren't born from eggs, Trish."

"Everything is born from eggs, stupid. I'm talking about *in vitro*. Embryos and crap. If someone at

U-GeneTech stole fertilized bloodhound eggs for them, all they would need are a few surrogates."

"I thought all female mods get sterilized before they're sold, to control the population."

"Yes, but female *humans* have birthed mods before."

"Yeah, regular-sized mods. You need synthetic wombs for the big ones, and you can't exactly buy those machines at the local hardware store. Wouldn't all the mothers die in childbirth?"

"Obviously. But some might say that's a small price to pay for giant, walking weapons."

"That's another thing," Ken switched the subject, supressing the thought of a war mod ripping through a woman's womb. "That mod was *huge* and it still snuck up on us. How could no one have noticed it until it was standing in the middle of the restaurant? I definitely didn't see anything."

"Well, you wouldn't have seen it coming. Somebody dropped it off with a truck or something."

"How do you know?"

"Because it escaped," said Trish. "The police can't find it, even with the MK9s sniffing after it. I checked, and its blood trail vanishes just a short ways from the restaurant. Meaning..."

"Someone picked it up, too," Ken realized with dread. "It was put there on purpose. But why? What kind of lunatic would unleash a war mod on the city?"

"Whoever it was, they didn't want it tracked back to them. I mean, it had no clothes, no collar, no markings... Not even its blood is traceable. Again, it could've come from anywhere."

"That doesn't really answer the question," Ken said, irritable in his exhaustion.

"Well, I don't know. It was probably some anti-mod group—again, like the Free Slaves. A lot of them died fighting the government's mods during the uprising. I bet they wanted to show the world how dangerous they are, so they let one loose to wreck shit up. But then your pretty doggy distracted it, and... Well, you know the rest," Trish breathed, looking at Yumi. "War mods aren't known for their intelligence. I don't blame it for chasing after her the way it did, and it's a good thing she was there, too. She saved a lot of lives yesterday, yours included."

"Yeah, but she almost died to do it," Ken said, gazing fondly at Yumi through the misty glass. "The doctor said some mods have this second, mutated adrenal gland that releases some chemical he called *wrathaline*. The chemical makes them extremely fast and strong, but their bodies try to destroy it with really high fevers, and their hearts can spasm or even burst from the stress. It's a miracle the heat didn't give her brain damage. For her to still be alive... She's one lucky girl."

He leaned on the cold, wet chamber, smiling over Yumi. Trish noticed his dreamy expression, and she sighed.

"And I suppose you think you're one lucky guy, huh?"

"Huh?" Ken grunted at Trish, blushing. "How so?"

"Don't play dumb," she said, smirking scornfully. "You're in love with your pet, aren't you?"

"For the last time, she's not my pet."

"Spin it any way you want, that doesn't change the fact that you bought yourself a girlfriend. How much does love cost, by the way?"

"See, I knew you'd react like this. Why do you think I kept her a secret?"

"I can think of a lot of reasons. Because you were ashamed. Because you knew you made a mistake. Because you didn't want me to know you bought a...*love slave*—"

"Oh, come on! A love slave? You don't know what you're talking about."

"I know you'd never make her work for nothing, meaning she probably sits at home all day, cooking and cleaning for you like some timid little housewife. Maybe some massages on the side?"

"I wish," he muttered. "She doesn't do any of that..."

"Then what does she do, exactly? Wait, let me guess: Comfort you? Kiss you? Fuck you?"

"No!" Ken barked, though she was half right. "I mean, we've kissed once or twice, but..."

"See?" Trish said smugly. "It's already begun. Pretty soon she'll be begging you for attention, snuggling with you whenever you sit down, sleeping next to you every night... Next thing you know, you'll find her waiting for you in bed, bare-ass naked."

"Yeah, right. That'll never happen," Ken said, blushing.

"You can argue all you want, but that's just how mods work. They might seem intelligent, but they only do what they were trained to do. My guess? She was bred to be the perfect girlfriend."

"The *what*?"

"Think about it. She was hot enough to seduce you, loyal enough to sacrifice herself for you, and strong enough to protect you, even from a war mod. Like I said, she's a love slave."

Ken pinched the bridge of his nose and sighed. "Assuming your crazy guesses are correct, what's your point?"

"Well, I doubt you'd sell her just because I asked you to, right?"

"Of course not," Ken said stubbornly.

"In that case...just be careful," said Trish. "She'll never truly love you, you know. She's a mod, and you're like one of those guys who would fall for a stripper if she called you cute. If you fall for her obvious lies, you're a gullible idiot, and you deserve what you get."

"So you're worried I'll get my heart broken? Is that it?"

"No. I'm worried you're so desperate you'd pay for love. I'm worried you'll throw away your money, your future, even your life over some bullshit romance with a goddamn *animal*."

"And so what if I do?" Ken fired back. "It's got nothing to do with you."

"It's got everything to—!" Trish caught herself, then ruffled her orange mane in aggravation. "I just don't get it, Ken. Why would you buy a mod?"

"I don't know. Maybe I was just tired of living alone. I was sick of serving ungrateful morons every day, slaving over a hot grill just to come home to an empty apartment. And for what? So I could save enough money to live alone somewhere else? Away from everything I know? Away from you?"

He made eye contact with Trish, but she gruffly turned away, glowing.

"Yumi is my chance to really mean something to somebody."

"You mean something to me," Trish mumbled. "I mean, if you hate living by yourself so much, why didn't you stay with me? You didn't need to buy a mod just because you were a little lonely."

"I know that, but...she needs me now, and...I think I need her too."

Trish exhaled, blowing her bangs out of her eyes. "Whatever. It's your money and your life. Waste them however you see fit."

"Thanks for understanding," Ken joked. "You know, I thought you'd be happy I was staying. Aren't you at least glad I'm not moving away?"

"I am," Trish said, rising. She strut toward the door, placing her hand on Ken's shoulder as she passed. "I just wish it was for a different reason," she said, then she patted him twice and departed.

Ken plopped himself back into the chair beside the cooling chamber, drained. After checking the monitor again, which now read 102.7, he let out a long, quiet breath and shut his heavy eyelids. He suddenly heard a soft, startling thump. Yumi wiped the moisture off the inside of her chamber. He wiped the dew off the outside, gazing into her vivid blue eyes through the clean pane. He pressed his hand against her pink pads and absorbed her warmth through the chilled glass. She smiled weakly, then retracted her faint touch, curling back to sleep.

"Don't listen to Trish," he said. "It doesn't matter what you were bred for. You can choose your own life now, and if you want a life with me, then I'll do everything I can to make you happy."

Yumi didn't respond, but he believed he saw her smile or nod slightly.

"We'll go home soon, okay? Let's go home..."

At around sunset that day, Yumi left the hospital sedated for a second time, though her light dose left her able to sway and stumble. Ken became her crutch, wearing her like a cumbersome coat. He helped her hobble in and out of a pod, up the elevator, and inside their apartment.

"Sorry about this," he said, kicking the front door closed. "I told them you weren't dangerous, but they wouldn't let me take you home unless they drugged you first."

She forgave him with a quick lick to his cheek.

"Are you still dizzy? Can you stand?"

He thought he felt her nod over his shoulder, so he gingerly set her down. Holding her hands like those of a toddler learning to walk, he guided her down the hallway toward the bedroom, but her legs buckled, and she woozily veered sideways, slamming into the wall and crumbling into a twisted heap. Not that it seemed to bother her, judging by her stupid grin.

"Okay, up we go," Ken said, pulling on her arms, but with her full, dead weight splayed out on the floor, he would never lift her six-foot frame. So he dragged her across the carpet. Her legs sparked with static electricity, and the friction tore her skirt down around her knees, but after struggling for about three minutes, he finally hoisted her lanky, uncooperative body up onto the mattress.

"All right," he panted, fixing her skirt back over her bottom. "Now, between your heart attack and all the wrathaline still floating around in your blood, you're just supposed to rest until your fever breaks. But don't worry; I'll take care of you until then, okay?"

Yumi vaguely nodded, while Ken touched her forehead. Her dry skin felt like a hot coffee mug.

"You're burning up again," he sighed. "You should really take a cold bath later, but drinking ice water will have to do for now. I'll be right back, puppy."

He petted her scruffy hair, before moving into the kitchen. He scoured the cupboards for his tallest glass, dumped eight ice cubes into it, and filled it to the brim with filtered, refrigerated water. Just then, strange shuffling emanated from down the hall. He anxiously returned to the bedroom.

"Yumi?" he called, but she didn't hear him over all her rustling.

Snuffling in his blankets, Yumi dizzily inhaled his scent, stretching and rolling across his bed, tangling her limbs up in his sheets. The distinct, heady smell of his sweat intoxicated her, and alluring moans seeped from her mouth, as she buried her face into a pillow and breathed deeply. Ken couldn't discern her actions through the sheets, but she may have been rubbing herself. Suddenly she noticed him gawking at her in the doorway, but rather than look embarrassed, she shot him a seductive leer, and she squeaked adorably, as if trying to speak.

Ken cleared his throat.

"I've got your, um, water," he said awkwardly, approaching the end table at her bedside, but before he could set the glass down, she burst from her comfy cocoon and wrapped her arms around his neck. Frigid water splashed across the floor, as she hungrily dragged him under the covers.

"Come on, Yumi," Ken half-heartedly protested. "You're drunk off your meds."

But she wouldn't relent. She pinned him and lapped at his face, soaking and warming his lips. She nibbled his neck, sending shivers of pleasure up his spine, then hugged him long and tight.

"All right, I get it," he said. "I'm glad you're safe, too."

He embraced her from underneath, sinking his fingertips into her supple leather vest. They snuggled, mushing their cheeks together, caressing. She lifted her head away, eyes and lips glistening. Yumi lowered her flushed face until their noses touched, and then she delicately kissed Ken, as all the power leaked out of her muscles. Her whole body went flaccid, except for her mouth and her weak, groping hands. Even if he wanted to take her, he knew she didn't have the strength for anything more than tender kisses, so he indulged and tickled her mouth until she fell asleep on his chest.

After sidling out from beneath her, Ken changed into his pajamas, set an alarm, snuggled into her, and joined her in unconsciousness. Every hour they woke to electronic screams, and he got her a fresh glass of water. She fussed, but she always guzzled every drop before passing out. Neither of them had slept much come morning, though Yumi stayed hydrated. Unfortunately, her fever didn't break. Her sweltering heat made Ken moist and ornery, yet he determinedly spooned with her until she regained enough energy to eat. That time came around noon.

"Feeling any better?" Ken asked her, as she groggily shuffled into the kitchen, sniffing at the savoury air. He flipped bacon, stirred eggs, and tossed bread into the toaster oven, but by the time he turned around, Yumi had disappeared. He heard rushing water through the half-open bathroom door. Just then, his smartphone rang and rattled on the countertop.

Busy cooking, he intended to ignore the call until he read the phone's screen: "Trish Holt."

He answered, "Hey?"

"It's official," Trish said cheerfully.

"What's official?"

"The restaurant is closing for at least a few weeks. A lot of our servers were injured in the attack, not to mention Max. We can't run a mod-themed restaurant without mods, right? Besides, that bloodhound wrecked up the lobby pretty good, so until the repairs are done and the mods heal up, we're on summer vacation! So, when are we finally gonna spend some time together, huh?"

"Um... I'm not sure. I'll have my hands full with Yumi for a while. Maybe next week?"

"Well, the rainy season's coming soon, and I wanna hit the beach before then, so—"

BA-THUMP! Alarming thuds resounded from the washroom, followed by the steady patter of the gushing showerhead—and distraught moaning.

"I'll call you back!" Ken cried, urgently ending the call, slapping his phone down on the table, and dashing into the washroom. Yumi lay dazed in the bathtub underneath the fallen shower curtain, whimpering and stirring, as artificial rain pelted her pallid face. Ken shut off the water.

"What happened, puppy?" he asked, with a cutesy, caring voice. "Did you faint again?"

She bobbled her head, eyes squeezed shut.

"Well, no wonder you're so weak; you haven't eaten anything in like a day. Come on, let's get you some breakfast." He grabbed her hand and pulled, but she shook her head, refusing to budge.

"What's the matter?" he asked, alarmed. "Did you break something?"

She shook her head again.

"Oh... You're just that dizzy, huh?"

She nodded, clutching the shower curtain like a security blanket.

"All right... I'll bring breakfast to you, then. Wait here," he said, as though she had the choice. He returned with a plate of lightly buttered toast, slightly burnt bacon, and overcooked eggs. "Sorry. I left it on the stove too long, but hopefully it's still good. *Here.*" He sat on the edge of the bathtub and passed the plate to her, but she didn't take it. Instead, Yumi opened her mouth wide.

"*Ahhhn...*" she squeaked suggestively.

"Oh. Do, uh...?" Ken nearly asked if she wanted him to feed her, but the answer was obvious.

Plucking a strip of bacon off the plate, he awkwardly extended the meat toward her gaping mouth, hand trembling. She chewed the tip, and he gradually pushed the strip deeper inside, until she gently nibbled his skin. Her lips clamped his fingers, and she licked them clean, lapping up the flavourful grease. It felt so strangely pleasant, he forgot the fork and fed her globs of egg by hand. Her slippery tongue tickled him, and her saliva warmed his fingertips, as her eyes and mouth begged him for more. An odd sense of disappointment struck him when she finished her food, but breadcrumbs covered her chest and chin, and butter and bacon grease soaked her lips.

He didn't need to ask. Yumi pointed to the faucet, handed him the washcloth she had brought into the tub with her, and—after a short, woozy struggle—pulled off the shower curtain. Ken had seen her naked once or twice before, but never in such an intimate, vulnerable way. As she stretched, he ogled her long, lean physique, from her fuzzy breasts, down the ridges of her taut stomach, to the mottled black and white thatch between her legs. Her eyes, bright and blue as sparkling sapphires, judged his expression, as if wondering, *"Do you like this weird body? Do you think I'm beautiful?"*

Their gazes connected, and their cheeks flushed pink. Speechless, Ken plugged the drain and turned the cold water tap to end the charged silence, splashing her feet. Rather than stare at her, he cleaned off her plate in the kitchen while the tub filled, settling his nerves with deep breaths, before returning to the washroom. Yumi shivered in the chilly bath, but the bracing water invigorated her mind and soothed her fever. She smiled up at Ken with chattering teeth, alert and expectant, as he kneeled on the discarded shower curtain, shut off the faucet, squirted shampoo into the washcloth, leaned over the tub, and—with another calming breath—washed her gorgeous body.

He scrubbed the cloth against her abdomen like a washboard, producing soapsuds. The belly rub relaxed her, and her shivering quieted, as his cloth travelled up between her breasts to her mouth. She pursed her lips while he washed off the grease, and when he used his bare hand to rinse off the foam, she playfully licked him. Next, against his better judgement, he moved straight to her breasts. Yumi flinched, so he hastily removed his hand, but she locked eyes with him and nodded. Erect from the cold, her pink nipples poked his palm through the washcloth. Full handfuls, her breasts felt larger than they looked, and when he squeezed, the plump, excess flesh bulged between his fingers.

Quelling his escalating excitement, Ken cleaned the less erogenous zones of her body: under her arms, over her knees, and down her shins. He massaged the sensitive pads on her feet and buffed her clawed toes, delaying the inevitable. As he tentatively scrubbed her thighs, approaching the thin pink slit hidden within her lush bush, Yumi may have sensed his unease, because she flipped over, presenting her bare back. Regaining some courage, he keenly traced her spine all the way down from her neck, then caressed the smooth curves of her ass. Abandoning the washcloth, he stroked the fine, silky hair on her fuzzy peach, but when he neared her crotch, his hands retreated up her tail.

In the end, Ken felt her every nook and cranny, except for one. He shampooed every inch of her luxurious tail, and he kneaded soap into her scalp, and he touched every pretty facet of her face, but ultimately, he denied himself, and her, the pleasure. However, as he ruffled her hair dry with a fluffy towel, she didn't appear dissatisfied. Rather, she still seemed lightheaded and on the verge of collapse, and he knew that he made the right choice. Only after she recovered could he allow himself to feel every private part of her body.

Fortunately, or unfortunately, depending on the perspective, Yumi remained too weak to care for herself over the next few days, granting Ken many more opportunities to feel every other part of her. He caressed her every morning during her chilly baths. He kissed her every night while they fell asleep. He stroked her every day when they watched television and movies. Without work to worry about, he invested in her full-time, spending every minute lounging in peace, bliss—and eventually boredom. Ken came down with his own fever—*cabin* fever—and Yumi started fidgeting and whining for no clear reason, but he knew she yearned to escape the cage they called home.

Despite her chronic fatigue, her temperature sat below 100 degrees, so Ken prepared them a picnic. She changed out of her vest into a breezy, baby blue dress, and they braved the searing sun, strolling hand-in-hand to the nearest park.

"This seems like as good a spot as any," he told her, spreading a blanket under the shade of a sprawling tree. Families and their dogs frolicked all around them, chasing rubber balls and catching plastic discs. Somewhat sheepishly, Ken pulled his own disc from the picnic basket. Yumi glowered at him, then the toy, then him again, narrowing her eyes thinner and thinner until she squinted.

She rapidly shook her head.

"Come on," Ken said, "some light exercise will be good for you."

She crossed her arms and harrumphed.

"*C'mon*. We may as well make a game of it, unless you'd rather just run around the park."

Yumi exhaled, pointedly turned her back on him, and then stomped away. After putting a fair amount of distance between them, she spun on her heel to face Ken, arms still firmly folded.

"You ready?" he called, winding up the disc.

She pouted, unresponsive, but he tossed it anyway. The disc sailed through the sky, caught a breeze, and curved to her left. She tracked its arc, unenthusiastically walking toward it, but when it swerved out of her reach, she panicked. With her arms crossed, she instinctively lunged—*"Ahhm!"*—biting the disc. As if to mock her, a nearby dog caught a disc in its mouth too.

Yumi's head drooped, and her cheeks glowed like pink neon bulbs. Humiliated, she shuffled over to Ken, dropped the disc at his shoes, and shuffled back.

"Don't use your teeth, then," he murmured, throwing the disc. It whirled toward her head like a buzz saw, as she absently kicked the grass, hands planted on her hips. Before Ken could warn her, her ears twitched, her head snapped up, and she reflexively—*"Ahhm!"*—bit the disc.

"Again!?" Ken blurted, dumbfounded.

Yumi pulled the toy out of her mouth and clutched it to her chest like an apologetic pauper fiddling with his tattered hat. She tossed it to Ken, then anxiously awaited his next throw, smoothing out the creases in her sundress to dry her sweaty palms. The disc flew back, slow and light and easy. Moving into position, she grasped for it with both hands. Beaming, she closed all ten fingers around the toy, and she caught it—*"Ahhm!"*—at the exact same time as a large, fluffy dog.

She blinked at the dog. He stared into her eyes. She shook her head. He nodded (seemingly), then he *ripped* the disc out of her fingers and bolted. Yumi gasped, and she chased him through the park, matching his pace. He worriedly glanced back at her, as he juked around a tree, over a bench, and through a cluster of playing children, but Yumi cleared the obstacles and then transitioned onto all fours, bounding after her prey. Her dress fluttered like a flag behind her, as she pounced, tackling the dog and rolling with him across the ground. She gripped the disc, and the dog clenched his jaw, and they engaged in a fervent, growling game of tug-of-war. Yumi quickly lost her patience and *chopped* him between the eyes. The dog yapped and skittered off, and she raised her toy high above her head like a trophy and laughed victoriously, "*Mwah-hah-heh-hah—!*"

"Hey!" yelled the dog's angry owner, storming toward her. "What do you think you're doing, attacking my dog?"

Yumi stuck out her tongue at him and ran away.

"Stupid mutt bitch!" the owner shouted after her. She flipped him her middle finger and raced back to Ken, who had watched the whole incident through his fingers while palming his face. Panting, she presented the disc to him like a golden medal.

"Are you proud of yourself?" he asked, tossing her plastic prize aside.

She chuckled mischievously, clasping her hands behind her back and twisting, and any shame or exasperation Ken felt toward her melted under her endearing smile. Suddenly her smile vanished, her legs trembled, and she tipped forward—

"Whoa!" Ken yelped, hurriedly cradling her body. He laid her down on their picnic blanket. "That's enough activity for one day, huh?" he said, as her head bobbled on his lap. Her shallow breaths concerned him, but her lucid gaze pacified his fear. She hugged him, nuzzling his abdomen, and he stroked her hair. Between the beaming sunlight, the fresh, clean scent of nature, and her sundress, Yumi had never appeared more sweet or feminine. He curled downward and kissed her warm cheek.

"You hungry yet?" he asked.

She nodded, inadvertently rubbing her head against his crotch. He plucked a puffy, powdered donut out of their picnic basket and offered it to her, but rather than grab it, she draped her hands across her stomach and opened her mouth. He indulged her, stuffing the puff into her slick pink hole. She munched on it until strawberry jelly oozed onto her tongue and lips, and when she finished, he kissed the powdered sugar off her mouth, covertly licking the liquid fruit out of the subtle fuzz on her face. Feeding her had quickly become one of his favourite activities.

"You know," Ken gulped, scratching his head, "this is sort of like our first real date, huh?"

Yumi nodded sleepily.

"S-so," he stammered, "I guess we're an official couple now."

Yumi nodded again.

"Am, uh...?" He cleared his throat, as insecurities swirled in his brain. "Do you...? I mean, um... Is this really want you want? Out of life, I mean. Are you really happy being my...you know?"

Yumi sat up, glared at him, and—"*Ow!*"—smacked him upside the head. Then she kissed him, as the dimming sun sagged on the horizon, and raw affection, absolutely absent of lust, swelled inside Ken. She lingered against his mouth, eyes wide open, and he breathlessly gazed back, searching...

Within a few days, Yumi's fever broke, and she regained her full, frisky, impulsive vitality. She and Ken made the most of his limited vacation time, frivolously dating on dwindling funds, as though they needed to complete some checklist: the romantic dinner date; the summer blockbuster date; the leisurely shopping date; and the thrilling sports date. One night, lounging in front of the television, Yumi pointed eagerly at a colourful commercial, suggesting their next date. Giant, luminous wheels, spinning, blinking chairs, and swooping metal snakes zoomed across the screen.

"Why're you all excited?" asked Ken. "Haven't you been to an amusement park before?"

Yumi shook her head, absorbing the ad through glittering eyes.

"It was pretty decent last year, when I went with Trish. I think they're setting up right now, actually. If all the upcoming rain doesn't cause too many delays, it should be done in about a week."

She pouted at him, as if to ask, *"What do you mean about a week?"*

"Hey, don't give me that look. It's an annual fair. Until they set up, there's nothing we can do. Well, there is a big theme park a few hours from here, but...I don't have a car. We may as well wait."

She sulked and kicked at Ken. Her playful actions led to a placating foot massage.

"We should get some sleep, though," he said. "We're meeting up with my sister pretty early."

Yumi whined about that, too, but the next morning, beneath the baking sun in her blue bikini, she grinned from ear to pointy ear, racing across the white sand toward the sparkling water.

"Don't run too far ahead!" Ken called, adjusting his grip on their towels, chairs, and bags.

"Just let her play," Trish said, slapping his naked back. "It'll give us a chance to catch up."

He faced her—*"Gwuh!"*—and nearly choked on his own saliva when he saw her swimsuit. Her sunglasses covered more skin. On top, tiny red triangles barely hid er nipples, and taut straps sunk into her flesh. Lower, past her firm stomach, another pair of triangles tried and failed to conceal her, plastered to her moist skin and tucked into her creases.

Involuntarily ogling her intimidating hourglass figure, Ken coughed.

"S-so, the whole time you drove us here, you were wearing *that* under your clothes?"

"What's the matter, kid?" she asked, leaning against his shoulder. "You don't like it?"

"You look like a porn star—*Ooph!*"

She punched him in the gut. He doubled over, scattering the towels and chairs over the sand. Trish snapped him into a headlock before he fell. Her huge warm boobs swayed against his face.

"What was that? I didn't quite hear you."

"N-nothing," he spluttered. "You look great. R-really cute. Sexy, even..."

She released him, and he dropped to his knees, desperately gulping up the humid air.

"Aww, that's sweet of you," she said facetiously, although she blushed.

"*I didn't mean it, you dumb cow,*" Ken mumbled, massaging his throat.

Oblivious to his insult, Trish grabbed their beach supplies and set them up close to the water. With every step she took, her bouncy utters almost overflowed, and her big round ass jiggled. Man glanced or outright gawked at her as she passed, and women smacked or scolded their boyfriends. Once Ken recovered, he brushed his sandy palms on his trunks and joined her. She lay on her belly across a towel, resting on her elbows and languidly kicking her feet.

"So fuckin' hot..." she sighed, watching Yumi splash and frolic. "Could you lotion my back?"

"Do it yourself."

Trish tipped her sunglasses down her nose to hit him with her full glower. "How the hell am I supposed to do that? Come on, don't be a wuss. Or are you afraid to touch a *real* woman?"

"Yumi is a—" he started, but quickly stopped. "Hold on..."

Ken plucked the sunscreen out of the bag, and then, perhaps because he was accustomed to caring for Yumi, he straddled Trish and squatted. Halfway down, he realized his mistake—too late. His legs cramped, straining to reverse his momentum, but he lost the fight and sat squarely on her ass cheeks. Surprise paralyzed her, but after three seconds of stunned silence, Trish joked, "Go ahead, make yourself comfortable."

Honestly, her squishy, heated cushions couldn't have felt comfier. So, after a short shrug, he squeezed lotion onto her bare back. She flinched at the cold squirt, but once Ken sunk his fingertips into her knotted muscles, she cooed and slackened. As he massaged her hot oily skin, he wondered how long it had been since he'd touched a woman's smooth, hairless body. He compared her rubbery flesh to Yumi's silky fur and couldn't decide which texture he preferred, though Trish certainly won in other areas. Even from behind, he could see her fat boobs, and he was pretty sure one of his nuts were lodged between her gelatinous cheeks. He controlled his breathing, struggling to keep soft.

"Hey," Trish said, "wouldn't it be funny if we made people think we're a couple?"

"Why?" he asked, rubbing near her shoulders, where her fiery hair tickled his hands. Her skin had long since absorbed the lotion. "They don't know we're related, so they wouldn't think it's weird."

"We're not related, though," she argued. "We're not even the same race."

"Exactly, so why would it be funny if people thought we were together?"

"Because we're *not* together."

"They don't know that!"

"Forget it, then!" Trish bellowed, burying her face in her towel. "It was a stupid idea, anyway. I'm probably not your type, or your species..."

"What are you trying to say?"

"Nothing," she exhaled. "Like I said, forget it."

Just then, an ominous shadow bathed Ken in cool darkness. He gazed up at the gathering grey thunderclouds on the horizon, though the sun shone high and unobstructed. Scratching his head, he turned toward the mysterious shadow—*"Gah!"*—and hastily climbed off Trish. Yumi scowled at him, arms crossed, tapping her foot.

"H-hey, Yumi!" he squeaked. "Where'd you come from?"

She didn't respond. Her icy eyes burrowed into his brain, injecting it with fear.

"Sorry, we're just really close!" he panicked. "Plus, she's not really my sister, so it's not weird! I mean, it's okay because we're related! I mean, uh... It's not what it looks like? *Ooph!*"

Yumi punched him in the gut, and he dropped. She ground her heel into his back and smirked down upon his suffering, as he twitched under her padded foot.

Why...? Ken thought, holding back tears. *Why are the women in my life so violent?*

"Nice punch," Trish said, rising to face Yumi. "He always was a little horndog. I told him no, but ever since we were kids, he's taken every excuse he can to put his grubby hands on me."

"You *lie*," Ken hissed, but she silenced him with a swift kick—*"Gwak!"*—to his ribs.

"You must be hot with all that fur," said Trish. Yumi eyed her suspiciously. "You wanna head over to the boardwalk and cool off with some ice cream? I'll tell you what Ken was like as a kid..."

Yumi nodded keenly. Trish hooked her arm around hers, and just like that they were off.

"Don't do it, Yumi!" Ken cried out. "She can't be trusted. Don't believe a word she says!"

Yumi ignored him, giggling at something Trish said, abandoning him on the sand.

"W-what just happened?" he wondered, coddling his bruised stomach.

After his crippling pain dissipated, Ken caught up to the women, apologized to them properly, and bought them assorted frozen delights. Trish whispered something to Yumi, and they giggled.

"What's this? Suddenly you're best friends?" he asked, as the vendor scooped out their treats.

"My problem was never with her," said Trish. "She's an innocent victim," she said, petting her shaggy hair. Yumi blinked at Ken, confused. He just shook his head, as if to say, *"Let it go..."*

He and Yumi shared a sundae, while Trish glared at them sideways, licking at her drippy ice cream cone, though her mood improved once they entered the water. They swam, racing to the buoys and back. With her superhuman strength, Yumi could've defeated them easily if she bothered to use any proper swimming techniques, but she dog paddled adorably, keeping the races close. Trish won more often than not, usually by pulling Ken's legs or dunking his head. At one point, as Yumi waited for them on the beach, they zealously wrestled for second place, spinning, groping, and splashing like crocodiles engaged in a death roll. During the intense battle, Trish's tiny top predictably slipped off. Rather than take advantage, however, Ken chivalrously retied her top while she hid her bare breasts, but the moment the race resumed, she yanked down his trunks and fled to open sand.

Trish and Yumi triumphantly high-fived, laughing, while he concealed himself underwater.

Later, after the sun disappeared behind a huge black cloud, Yumi dug a deep hole in the sand barehanded. She dragged Ken over to it and proudly pointed at her work. He reluctantly sat inside.

"Is burying things fun for you or something?" he asked, while she filled the hole up to his neck. Good and stuck, he sat there, buried and bored, until Yumi got down on her belly and inched toward him, wearing a naughty smile. "Whatever embarrassing thing you've got planned, *don't*—!"

She *licked* his cheek. He scrunched up his face and squirmed, but the sand weighed down his limbs, trapping him underground. Her greasy tongue slid over his clenched eyelid.

"All right, that's enough!" Ken bleated, bright red.

Trish lay on her stomach beside Yumi.

"That actually looks kinda fun," she said playfully to Yumi. "Do you, uh, mind if I join you?"

Yumi shook her head, grinning.

"No!" Ken cried, but Trish pecked his brow and tapped her lips to his cheek, at least keeping it innocent. *"Uunnnnahh!"* He groaned nonetheless, struggling. The women kissed and slurped at him, wetting his face, giggling at his distress—

K-KRAKOOM! Suddenly lightning struck, and the clouds burst. The gentle patter of raindrops soon became a roaring deluge, soaking the beach and everybody on it. The white sand turned brown, the towels turned soggy and useless, and Ken turned crabby, as the rain washed the saliva off his face.

"I'd like to get out now," he said, expressionless.

The women gave him one last kiss to cheer him up. Yumi clawed through the damp sand until she could hook her hands under his arms, and then she plucked him out of the ground like a carrot.

On the long, drowsy ride home, Ken spotted six vehicles in the flooded ditches. Frequent flash flood warnings for city zones crackled through the radio, and whenever thunder shook the weeping sky, Yumi flinched and huddled into Ken. They cuddled in the backseat, trusting Trish to traverse the shallow rivers the street became, until she safely dropped them off at their apartment.

Following a lovely meal of crisp salad, baked salmon, and white wine, Yumi washed up while Ken cleaned up. When she moved into their bedroom to dress, she left a startling amount of sand in the bathtub, but he put up with the pebbles during his shower, too exhausted to do more than guard the drain with his feet. Wearing only his towel, he grumbled all the way to the bedroom, intending to scold Yumi—but when he saw her, his thoughts and irritation evaporated.

She sat on the edge of their bed, holding two glasses of brandy, wearing only her golden collar. His eyes roamed from her slender feet, up her strong, crossed legs, over her bare breasts, to her sinful smile. She motioned to the bottle of brandy on the nightstand, then offered him a glass.

Ken indecisively looked into her eyes. For a moment, the only noises came from the raindrops drumming on the windows, the blood pounding in his ears, and the saliva squelching down his throat. Questions and confusion flitted through his mind like flustered hummingbirds: *Are we ready? This is her choice. She wants to do this, but do I? If we do this, there's no going back. Are you ready? If it'll make her happy, I should do it. Should I say something? This is so sudden. Am I ready?*

"Yumi..." Ken began, but she cut him off with a determined nod. She got up off the mattress, wary of spilling their drinks, and kissed him long and hard, luring him backward with her lips, until she sat back down, and he took a glass from her. Nervous, he drained his drink, glancing at the ceiling, as she languorously reclined on her elbow, sipped at her brandy, placed her feet against his stomach, and removed his towel with her toes. It flopped to the floor, and he dangled before her eyes.

Ken watched the rain pelt the windows, flushed and lightheaded. Something spongy pressed his exposed worm against his abdomen, and soothing heat engulfed his brain. He finally looked down. Yumi gazed up at him, equal parts thrilled and humiliated, squashing his gradually thickening penis against his body with the squishy pads on her soft soles. Her rubbery paws rubbed his shaft, and her clawed toes cautiously wiggled against his head, and her tongue ladled booze into her mouth, as she panted into her glass, fogging the inside. Ken smiled empathetically at her anxiety, supressing a laugh.

They set their glasses aside, and when Ken turned back, Yumi pinched his cock between her thumb and forefinger, careful not to scratch it. Her slimy tongue slid through her lips and slathered the tip. Spasms of pleasure shot through his spine, as she dragged her tongue down his twitching dick and over his raised veins. She lapped the gooey dew off the top, tasting his essence, and then stuffed his cock into her mouth. Ken played with her ears and petted her head, as she slurped and gently nibbled. She growled, and for a split second the absurd thought that she might bite him crossed his mind, but she suddenly popped his engorged meat out of her mouth and splayed herself across the sheets. She displayed her belly, as if surrendering, but her fierce eyes told him loudly, *"Your turn, boy. Do what you want with me!"*

He obeyed, but not before he fully repaid her. Impassioned, he swigged a mouthful of brandy straight from the bottle, swallowing one burning half, and then he crawled on top of Yumi and kissed her deeply, force-feeding her the rest. Plum liquid trickled from the corners of their mouths, and she licked the stinging juice off his gums, before he travelled to her breasts. He fondled them, squeezing her fuzzy warm flesh until she squeaked in pain, then he took one of her nipples between his lips, as his fingers snuck down between her legs. He found her hot, slick slot, and he jammed a finger inside. She clamped his finger and gasped. He slowly slid in and out, and when her hole slackened, he shoved another finger inside and pushed his thumb into her clit. Fluid seeped out of her, as Ken rubbed the rough patch within her and sucked on her nipple until it glowed red. She hugged his whole head, convulsing each time he lightly bit or grazed her sensitive buttons.

He removed his sticky fingers, delirious, wondering how she tasted, but rather than lick his own hand, he went straight to the source. Kissing her moist lower lips, her sour, feminine scent rose from her like steam, and carnal hunger seized his senses. He peeled the hood off her swollen clit and sucked, swallowing her tangy lube. The pleasure overcame her, and she wiggled away, so he pursued her across the bed. They wrestled and rolled until he lay beneath her. She sat, resting her wet pussy on his mouth. He flexed his tongue, flicking and stabbing up at her, while she fidgeted and moaned, squeezing him between her thighs. She kneeled off of him, and he gasped for fresh air. Thin webs attached his chin to her crotch, and once he caught his breath, she sat down again. He tensed his lips against her clit and vigorously shook his head side to side, and back and forth, and in tight circles. She gripped his hair. Her entire body curled around his head. Yumi squealed, and her warm fluids surged out over his face.

After he crawled out from under her and wiped his mouth clean with the sheets, Ken beheld a breathtaking view. On her knees, Yumi panted, staring back at him over her shoulder. She massaged and spread her gaping, leaking hole. Her unwavering eyes begged him, *"Fuck me! Fuck me now!"*

Doggy style, eh? Ken thought, nearly chuckling.

Like a starving wolf, he crept behind her. She wagged her tail against his chest, brushing him like a feather duster. He grabbed her waist and prodded his bulging cock against her tender hole, wetting the tip. Yumi screamed—*"Ayahhh!"*—when he plunged his rigid pole deep into her pussy. She clutched the sheets and buried her face into his pillow, inhaling his scent, and he thrust out, then in, and out, then in, steadily pumping faster and faster until the bed rocked, and the mattress squeaked almost as loud as she did, and his hips loudly slapped against her ass.

Her rippled walls closed around his cock, crushing him like a vise. She drooled, and her eyes rolled back into her skull. *"Aghwuu!"* Yumi gurgled, sinking her fangs into his pillow. Ken gripped the base of her bushy tail and slammed his steely dick into her again, again, *again*. She shuddered and shouted. He worried about the thin walls and the neighbors, but her heady smell, and the fruity booze, and her sweet squawks drove him into a frenzy.

Ken scraped the juice out of her vagina, cramming himself into every fold of her constricting tube, and she tore mouthfuls of foam out of his pillow, groaning. Her strong legs quavered, and she collapsed, so he fell into her, clutched her boobs, and ploughed her, pounding every tingling inch of himself into her snug cunt. She cried, *"Kwuagh!"* He snarled, and on a whim, he slid his tongue against her bristly face. Something dormant inside him ignited. He kissed her everywhere his lips could reach, and with a loud, rough growl, he spewed hot cream into her cramping tunnel. They howled together, melding into one. Yumi ripped his pillow to pieces, whimpering, as Ken chewed on her leathery ear, hugging her so hard he thought he might crush her.

After they finished twitching and wheezing, Ken flipped her over and remained tucked inside her, unable to relinquish her womanly warmth. He embraced her, pecking her neck. A noise between a laugh and a sob escaped her lips, and she crackled as best as she could, "*Keh...hnn...*"

Tears stung his eyes. He stroked her, speechless.

"*Khe...nn,*" she spoke again, a little more clearly. "*Ke...n.*"

"Yumi," he said, kissing her forehead. She licked his throat. "Yumi..."

Love and lust struck him like the lightning raging beyond their windows. They snuggled while he gradually grew longer and stronger inside her body, breathing heavily. The second he could spear her hard enough to make her moan again, he plowed into the viscous cream he'd packed inside her, and she lapped at his face, and soft squelching noises echoed throughout the room.

"*Ken,*" she said, fuelling his desire.

"*Yumi,*" he said, licking her cheek.

They whispered, called, and cried each other's names until their bodies ached and wilted.

Knock! Knock!

Ken awoke to booming thunder, drumming raindrops, and sharp knocking.

Knock! Knock! Knock!

In absolute darkness, he climbed out of bed, accidentally bumping and waking Yumi.

"*Ueh?*" she mumbled. He interpreted her noise as, "What is it? Is something wrong?"

"It's okay. Go back to sleep, puppy. If anyone's here this late, it's Trish." A sudden thunderclap reminded him of the flood warnings he heard on the radio. "Do you think her house was flooded?"

Yumi grunted something. He patted her bum, and she stretched, slowly inhaling through her nostrils. He lurched upright, pulled on some pajama bottoms, and stumbled from the room.

Yumi sniffed, snuffled, and urgently rustled.

"*Ken!*" she whispered, calling him back to bed.

"One second, puppy."

Knock! Knock!

"I'm coming already!"

Yumi yelped too quietly, just before he unlocked and opened the front door.

Ken squinted into the light pouring in from the doorway, gaping at his visitors in shock. All fatigue fled his brain. Adrenaline shot through his blood, and he hastily slammed the door—*BANG!*—but something bashed it back open, tossing him across the floor. A man wearing a black raincoat and metallic mask calmly walked into the apartment, hands hidden inside his pockets. Ken gawked at the familiar figure behind the bizarre stranger and gasped. The figure crawled through the doorway, too tall to fit otherwise. One massive arm squeezed through, then a head missing one floppy ear.

"Can you smell her, Chopper?" the man melodically asked the bloodhound. He inhaled deeply, perhaps catching whiffs of booze and sweaty interspecies sex off of Ken, and he laughed. "I can..."

Ken glared up at the masked man. The steel face of a snarling dog stared back.

CHAPTER FIVE

"How can you still smile?"

Ken crawled backward and bumped into the sofa. The bloodhound called Chopper clawed through the doorway, scratching out strips of carpet. He now wore something like a tarp around his waist. A flash of lightning illuminated the rolls of stained bandages wound around his wounds. Like an undead warrior rising from its tomb, Chopper dragged himself into the apartment, shut the door, and sat beside his master—a man with a drenched raincoat and a dog's metal face.

"Where's my girl?" he asked, in a flamboyant, melodic voice. "Where's my Nayela?"

"N-nayela?" Ken repeated, staring vacantly into his mask. "Who...?"

"Never mind," the man sighed, flicking his head sideways. "Check the bedroom, Chopper. Oh, and try not to get yourself killed."

Chopper warily prowled through the hallway, flicking light switches and smelling the air.

Ken finished his earlier question. "W-who are you?"

"Who? I figured someone with your tastes would recognize this face." He tapped the crinkled nose on his mask—*Ting, ting*. "Oh, well. Allow me to introduce myself. My fans call me *The Breeder*."

Suddenly a loud crash echoed from the bedroom, and The Breeder hurried to investigate. Ken crept into the kitchen and grabbed a knife. He urgently joined the scuffle to rescue Yumi, but when he saw Chopper rip the sheets, flip the bed, and tear the clothes out of the closet, he knew she had somehow escaped. All the windows appeared closed, confounding her stalkers, but he expected that she covered her tracks. Sure enough, when Ken checked the murky window that led to the fire escape, remnants of raindrops wet the sill. Seconds later, two blue eyes peeked at him through the pane.

Run, Yumi! Ken thought, furtively waving her away. *Go! Get out of here!*

She ducked out of sight. He couldn't be certain where she went, if anywhere, but if she simply sat outside the window, he needed to distract her pursuers before they realized her escape route.

"Damn it!" hissed Breeder. "Did we just miss her? Did she smell us coming?"

Ken considered stabbing him in the back, but Chopper would've slaughtered him in response. So, instead, he hid his knife behind his leg and said, "Whatever you want, take it and leave."

"She was here," Breeder insisted, removing a wadded pair of lacy underwear from his pocket. He held them up for Chopper. "Is this the right place, boy? Is this the room?"

Chopper snuffled the panties, rubbing his nose in the crotch, then he ripped a semen-stained sheet off the overturned bed and took a long, deep breath. He came away growling, and he glowered at Ken with something like jealousy in his beady eyes, before he nodded.

"That's what I thought," said Breeder, tucking the underwear away, before facing Ken. "So, what was my mod doing in your bed, huh? Did you fuck my girl?"

"I don't own any mods."

"Don't lie! You've got women's clothes in your closet, and there's fur all over your bed." He swiped the blanket from Chopper to show Ken the dark hairs clinging to the cloth. "Unless you shed, she was *here*! So, where is the bitch?"

Ken gnashed his teeth. "She likes to go for walks."

"In this weather? This late?"

"I guess so. She just leaves, sometimes for hours. I don't know where she goes."

"*Tch!*" The man tossed the sheet. "If that's true, her scent could be scattered all over the city," he mused. "And I can't exactly wander the streets looking for her, not with Chopper... Where are you, Nayela?"

"I don't know any Nayela. What do you want with my girlfriend?"

"She's not *yours*!" Breeder screeched, lunging at Ken. Ken tightened his grip around his knife, steeling himself to kill another man. Breeder reached for his throat with a gloved hand, and his blade flashed—but Chopper swiftly snatched his master away. Ken stabbed empty air and lost his balance, then—*WHACK!*—Chopper backhanded him, and he flew through the doorway, skipped like a pebble down the hall, rolled across the living room, and slammed into the wall. The world flashed white. He drooled blood and crumpled, and just when he fought onto his hands and knees, a hard boot crashed into his stomach, lifting him off the floor. Red mist sprayed from his mouth. The Breeder gripped his short hair and ripped his head back, then pressed the cold kitchen knife to his neck.

"I should slit your throat," he said, "but if she comes back and finds you dead, she'll just run, and I'd rather not risk her slipping away. So, you're going to be my hostage. Doesn't that sound fun?"

"I told you, I don't know your Nayela."

"And I told you not to lie!" The man stomped on his head, grinding his face into the carpet. "Chopper's nose is never wrong."

"Maybe my mod just smells like yours," Ken said cheekily, bracing himself for another blow, but Breeder stepped off him, slapped his knife on the coffee table, and grabbed the controller for the television. He casually turned it on, switched from TV, to Movies, to Web, and then he rapidly typed something on the tablet. Ken blearily crawled toward the knife, but Chopper almost crushed his arm beneath his heel. The bloodhound snarled at him, then stepped backward, as if to say, "Try that again. I dare you."

Ken nearly chuckled at the surreal situation, watching this masked lunatic leisurely surf the net on his couch. Just then, agonized moans breached the silence and swam into his ringing ears. He recognized the voice, the squawks of pained pleasure, and dread clutched his lungs.

"Are you certain you've never seen this girl?" asked Breeder.

Against his instincts, Ken faced the screen. Chained and muzzled, Nayela whined and writhed, as The Breeder, naked except for his metal dog mask, fucked her from behind. He yanked her leash, making her arch her back and gag.

"Remember her now?" he asked, rapidly cycling through clips.

In the next vile video, Breeder humped her leg and squirted into her fur. In the next, she licked his semen out of a doggy bowl and then pissed on a patch of turf. In the next, he pushed a big rubber bone into her asshole, while she bit down on a squeaky chew toy to withstand the anguish.

"Remember her now?" Breeder repeated, after every appalling clip. "Remember her now?"

For what seemed like hours, Ken gawked at the screen, numb. Cold shock trickled through his mind, but once his rage sparked, it exploded into a terrifying inferno that engulfed his heart and soul. "This is...!" he choked, curling his fingers into fists. "You...!" he seethed, sipping air through his teeth. "*GRAAAGH!*" he snapped, launching toward the knife, but Chopper slammed his palm into his spine—*Bwoom!*—pinning him to the floor.

Ken yelled unintelligibly, cursing, wriggling under Chopper's hand like a bug under a rock.

"Ooh?" Breeder giggled, lounging across the sofa. Thunder rattled the windows. "Did that last one jog your memory? And here I thought you'd enjoy my work."

"You sick fucking rapist bastard!" said Ken.

"Rape is such an *evil* word. She could be a bit reluctant, but few slaves truly enjoy their work. Anyway, after a little convincing, she always consented."

"Yeah, right after you threatened and tortured her, I bet. I've seen her scars! What did you do? Shock her every time she refused? Starve her until she let you fuck her? But as long as she nodded, you could do whatever the hell you wanted to her, huh?"

"That's what the law says." He laughed over the moans from the television. "Mods exist to be slaves. It doesn't matter if you use them for hard labour or hardcore porn. You can discipline them if they disobey. You can kill them if they fight back. And as you pointed out, you can fuck them bloody so long as they nod their pretty heads. Those are the rules. Can you blame me for playing along?"

"The rules also say I'm allowed to kill you for invading my home," said Ken. "And believe me, I plan on playing along."

"You aren't in any position to threaten me," Breeder said. Chopper pressed Ken into the floor to stress the point. "Even if you tattle on me, I'll just buy my way out of trouble like I always do. The fact is, nobody cares about the lives of a few mods. Yes, I sometimes punish my slaves, but so do the police. I heard they executed an MK9 in front of a crowd a few weeks ago. Apparently it attacked an officer. Tragic. If I killed my girls every time they nipped at me, I'd have a pile of dead whores."

"You mean you have other girls?"

"Of course. I don't usually brag, but I produce the best mod porn in the world. It's my art form. I have more subscribers than any other mod site. Millions of fans enjoy my work every month. Again, I'm surprised you didn't recognize my face—"

"Shut up already!" Ken yelled, digging his fingers into the carpet. He clawed forward an inch. Chopper pushed down on his back. "I'm tired of hearing your fucking voice. You raped Yumi..."

"Who?"

Ken wormed forward another few inches, chafing his belly. "You broke into our home..."

"You let me in, actually."

"You attacked us..."

"Only you. And you tried to stab me, remember?"

"I said, shut up!" Ken bellowed, eyeing the knife. It still rested almost a foot out of his reach. "I might not be able to rescue your other girls, but I will save Yumi. I'll kill you, even if it kills me!"

Ken lunged forward, reaching so far he thought the skin over his ribs would rip. He grasped the nearest wooden leg of the coffee table and yanked on it—*CRACK!* The leg snapped, the table titled, and the knife slid down the slope into his waiting hands.

Breeder gasped, but Chopper gripped Ken and smashed him up against a wall. The television crashed to the ground, shattering. Yumi's cries ceased. Ken jabbed the blade into Chopper's fingers, chipping at the bones, but the beast clutched his arm. Chopper squeezed. Ken dropped his knife and screamed, and his arm creaked, as the pressure gradually built. Chopper laughed cruelly, anticipating the impending *snap*, but just before he crushed Ken's bones, Breeder shrieked, "STOP, CHOPPER!"

Baffled, the hound spun to find Yumi standing behind the couch, nude and dripping wet, with her claws around his master's throat. She pressed her fingernails into the rigid cartilage of Breeder's trachea. He swallowed, and his throat shifted, and thin trails of blood leaked down his neck.

"Drop him, boy," he said, raising his arms in surrender. "Now!"

Chopper obeyed. Ken flopped to the carpet and then scrambled over to Yumi.

"Damn it," said Breeder. "Was she always here? How did she get inside?"

"The fire escape in the bedroom," said Ken. "You were too busy rambling to notice, but I had a clear view down the hall. All I needed to do was distract your pet long enough for her to reach you."

"So, what now? Are you going to kill me?"

"We should, but I doubt your buddy over there would let us get away with it."

Chopper growled and flexed, busting some of the bandages off his scabby, bulging muscles.

"So we're going to wait for the police," said Ken. "If the neighbors haven't already called about the noise, there's a station with MK9s just up the street. Once I call the cops, they'll be here in minutes. In other words, you're finished—!"

Breeder abruptly laughed. His smug chuckle escalated to a desperate, manic cackle, and then he yelled, "Wrong! In other words, the bitch rips out my throat, and we all die tonight, or she lets go, and *he* lets you live."

"W-what?"

"You said it yourself. If you kill me, Chopper will hunt you down. You'll be dead by the end of the night. But, Nayela..." Breeder said, staring up at her through the dark holes in his mask. "If you let me go, I might still drag you back home, but at least your new boyfriend won't have to die. *Chopper,*" he sang. "If she doesn't release me on the count of three...kill them both."

"*Shit!*" Ken cursed, glancing at Yumi. She clenched her teeth and stiffened.

"One..." said Breeder.

"Let him go, Yumi," Ken said reluctantly. "If you kill him, we die."

"Two..."

"You don't have to go back. We can run!"

"Three!"

"*GWOOOOOAR!*" Chopper launched at Yumi.

Time seemed to freeze. In that terrifying second, Yumi's brain devised two choices: *kill or flee.* Panicked, she picked both. She grabbed her lover's arm and bolted, dragging her fingertips across her abuser's throat. She only shaved off some skin, but The Breeder squealed nonetheless. Halfway down the hall, Yumi realized she smiled.

"*GROOUGH!*" Chopper crawled after her, banging against the tight walls and low ceiling. Her smile vanished. She flew with Ken through their bedroom to the open window. They climbed out into the rain onto the fire escape, and just as they started clamouring down the steel staircase, a giant arm *punched* through the window. Debris and water poured over them, as they ran three storeys down to the alley where they first met. They dashed past the dumpster to the street, their bare feet splashing in deep puddles, and as they rounded the building, Ken hoped to see swirling lights or hear sirens. No luck. The only vehicle in sight was a large unmarked moving truck parked across the street.

My neighbours must be heavy sleepers, he thought, just before he heard a sharp *CRASH* from above. He and Yumi gazed up toward the noise, then hastily ducked away. Glass shards rained to the pavement, and then— *BOOM!*—Chopper landed hard enough to crack the concrete. Breeder hopped down off his broad back, his black raincoat billowing in the storm. Lightning crackled across the sky.

"Come home, Nayela!" Breeder rasped over the rolling thunder, clutching his wounded neck. "I don't want to hurt you, you know. You were my favourite girl."

"You don't care about her!" spat Ken, backing away with Yumi. "Why are you so desperate to get her back, anyway? What does she know that your *fans* already don't? What are you afraid of?"

"Why would I be afraid? I'm just like most slave owners. Even if she had anything on me, any proof at all, she can't speak. She can't read or write. She's an illiterate idiot, only good for fucking."

"Then why go through all this? You have other girls. Why can't you just leave her alone?"

"Because she's *mine!*" the creep screeched. "She might be just a whore, but she's *my* whore! Before I bought her, she was training to be a *soldier*. If I hadn't saved her, she would've died like a dog in some senseless war. I couldn't let this rotten country waste her like that. I mean, look at that face, that body. Just look at how beautiful she is..."

Ken carefully peddled backward, nearing an intersection with Yumi.

"You just pulled her out of one hell and sent her to another," he said, as a lone pod approached. "Instead of turning her into a weapon, you made her your toy."

"As long as she listened to me, I treated her like a princess," said Breeder. "She would've been happy, if she only *listened*! But she's still my girl. She belongs to me. And I'm taking her back."

"She's not your toy," Ken said, glancing at the road. "She was never yours. You're insane!"

"No," The Breeder said, suddenly calm. "It's this world that's insane. I'm only playing along." He flicked the blood off his leather glove, then pointed at his prey. "Chopper? Sic 'em, boy..."

The beast lumbered like a living corpse, his soggy bandages peeling off his gooey scabs.

"*RWUAAGH!*" Chopper charged, but he'd never catch Yumi. Ken had stalled long enough. As if sharing the same thought, the lovers frantically sprinted for the pod currently parked at a red light. On green, it would zip away faster than any mod could possibly run, but Ken ran considerably slower than any mod. Chopper gained on him, making up meters of ground with every bound. The opposite light turned yellow. Ken neared the pod, and the beast pounced. Yumi suddenly leaped between them and snarled, and she *screamed*, fur bristling, and Chopper instinctively reeled back, perhaps recalling how she chewed off his ear. The light turned green. Yumi snatched Ken's wrist, stretched out for the pod, and— *SHINK!*—punctured its hull with her fingers, just as it zoomed off, nearly ripping her arm out of its socket.

Ken dangled from Yumi, scraping his feet on the asphalt. He hugged her waist, freeing up her other hand, and then she scaled the pod with her claws like an adept mountain climber, hoisting them onto the roof. Her legs flapped behind her like flags. Raindrops pelted her like liquid bullets, and the turbulent G-forces tried to pry off her hands, but she held on tight, terrified and exhilarated, until the pod eventually stopped. They slid down, waved to the bewildered passengers that had inadvertently rescued them, and ran to the nearest kiosk to order their own ride. Hands shaking, Ken took five minutes to input his info.

Chopper never caught up.

Without any money or clothing, save for a soaked pair of pajama pants, Ken and Yumi arrived at Trish's house, a small blue suburban abode. Ken pounded on the door and the doorbell for a few minutes. She answered angrily, "What the fuck do you want?" But when she saw them drenched and naked, she knew the severity of the situation. She called the police while they toweled off and put on dry clothes. Ken found jeans that fit him fairly well, and when he slipped on an old shirt that Trish often wore to bed, her scent enveloped him like a warm hug, and tears stung his eyes. His breath and hands shivered, but when he heard the police knock, he supressed his anxiety to give his report.

Expressionless, Yumi curled up under a blanket on the couch, while Ken explained everything from the heinous abuse The Breeder broadcast online to the most recent blatant kidnapping attempt.

"If this *Breeder* guy knows where you live, you might not want to go back until he's caught," one of the officers told them. After promising to look into it, he escorted them home, though only so they could somberly pack some clothing and hygienic supplies for their temporary stay with Trish.

That night, like a scared child after a nightmare, Ken slept between his big sister and his dog, quietly weeping. In the stifling darkness, he felt small and weak beside the two tall, strong women.

"You can only handle so much on your own," Trish whispered, when she heard him sniffle. "I'll help you get through this, okay?"

"I didn't want to drag you into this," Ken said, his voice thick with stress.

"Hey... If anyone picks on you, I'll kick their ass. Just like when we were kids."

Ken laughed sadly, and Yumi embraced him, apparently awake. She licked a tear off his face.

Damn it, he thought. *What kind of man am I? Why is she the one comforting me?*

They readjusted, and he spooned with her, careful not to crush her tail. He tucked her bottom into his hips, but guilt pierced his brain, so he lay flat on his back to stare at the ceiling. Yumi flipped over and assertively rested her shaggy head on his chest, as if to say, *"Deal with it."* For some reason, Ken pulled Trish close too, roughly hugging her with one arm. He felt strangely relieved.

Both women passed out on top of him, but he stayed awake, smoldering with fear and fury. He didn't even care when his arm fell asleep under Trish. Whenever he closed his eyes, he pictured that masked psychopath defiling Yumi, and whenever he considered her painful past, grief burned beneath his sternum, and his tears returned. And whenever he recalled kissing her, touching her, *fucking* her, remorse stung his heart like a hornet.

Someone shook him awake. Sunrays beamed through the blinds. Ken stirred and blinked, and when he finally focused on Trish, he noticed she was already washed and dressed for the day.

"Get your ass up," she said, leaving the room. "Your breakfast'll get cold."

Ken felt around for Yumi and grabbed nothing but blankets. He listened to the sound of rain beating on the roof, wondering how long it had been since he had woken up alone. Heart pounding, he climbed out of bed and staggered from the room, down the hall, into the open layout of the house. Trish carried a plate of pancakes around the short wall dividing the kitchen from the dining and living rooms and placed it on the table between the sausages and scrambled eggs. Ken scanned the empty chairs and couches, then glanced back toward the vacant bathroom, scratching his bare chest.

"Where's Yumi?" he asked Trish.

"Backyard," she said, returning to the kitchen to grab dishes from the cupboards.

Ken looked to the backdoor. Yumi's black leather vest hung on the coatrack, and the rest of her outfit rested in a pile on the floor.

"Is she naked out there or something?"

"Almost," Trish said, setting the table. "At least she's not out front."

Curious and concerned, Ken moved into the backyard. Bathing in the cool rain, Yumi sprawled on the sodden grass in her collar and panties, gazing up at the clouds. She appeared tranquil. He knelt beside her. She glanced at him, then went back to staring at the sky. Her eyelids flinched whenever a raindrop smacked her face, but she otherwise didn't budge.

"Do you, um...like the rain?"

Yumi nodded, rubbing the back of her head in the mud.

"I guess your last owner didn't really let you outside much, huh?"

She shook her head, then rubbed her eyes. He hadn't noticed because of the rain, but she was crying. He stroked her hair, soothing her the only way he knew how. His eyes stung. He blinked, and a warm raindrop trickled down his cheek.

"I'm sorry, puppy," he said. "I'm so sorry... I should've known. I should've realized sooner..."

The signs were there, he thought. He knew she'd been abused, but he hadn't considered how. Perhaps he simply didn't want to think about it.

Smiling softly, Yumi reached up and cupped his cheek. *"It's not your fault,"* she seemed to say. *"You couldn't have known."*

Ken took her hand and pressed her fingers to his lips.

"How?" he whispered. "How are you so strong? How can you still smile?"

Yumi carefully tapped her claw to his chest. "Ken," she spoke. Then she grabbed his wrist and placed his palm between her breasts, so he could feel her heartbeat. *"It's because of you,"* she told him, without speaking another word. *"I can smile again because of you..."*

Ken bent low and pressed his forehead against hers. He rubbed her ear, keeping one hand over her heart. The beat reassured him. He kissed her brow, like a father putting his daughter to bed.

"Hey, lovebirds!" Trish shouted from the backdoor. "I didn't cook all this for myself!"

They went back inside, dried off, and joined Trish. Ken mostly ate in silence, deep in thought. Trish noticed how he poked at his food like a sullen little boy sentenced to a night of homework.

"Stop pouting, all right? The police will catch that guy. There's nothing to worry about."

"If that was true, we wouldn't be hiding from him," said Ken. "They didn't catch his war mod. If he tracks her here..."

"He won't," Trish said, chewing a clump of egg. "It's not like that monster of his can just walk around in plain sight sniffing for her. He probably drives it around in his truck all slow, letting it smell the air as he goes. You know, like finding a small word in a big word search."

"Here we go with your theories again. How would Chopper track us from inside a *truck*?"

"I don't know. Maybe he knocks on the walls to tell his owner where to turn. But you live on a major street. What are the chances he'll drive way out here in the suburbs?"

Ken simply shrugged.

"Think about it," said Trish. "It took him about a *month* to find your place. And that Chopper probably only found her at the restaurant because she was out in the open on a main road."

Ken sighed, already weary of her wild speculation.

"Believe me," she said, buttering her pancakes, "the police will find him before he finds us."

"I don't know if we can even trust the police. The Breeder told me something like, 'I can just buy my way out of trouble again.' I'm pretty sure he's been bribing people, who knows for how long."

"That might be, but there's no way he's bribing the whole police force. Nobody's that rich. He's probably just paying the few people assigned to his case or something."

"I guess," Ken said pensively. "I mean, he seemed pretty freaked out when I threatened to call the cops— but if he's as popular as he says he is, the police already know about him for sure. It's not like he's growing weed in his basement. The guy plasters his crimes all over the Internet."

"Well, mod porn isn't automatically illegal. Until *she* ran away, there might not have been any reason to believe his girls were doing it against their will. Hell, some of them might even enjoy it. Er, no offence."

Yumi glared across the table at Trish and chomped a sausage in half.

"I'm just saying, things are different now," said Trish. "It's not just a few mods having sex on camera. The police know he's abused one of his girls. They know he owns the mod that killed Max, and they *know* he attacked you. Like I said, stop worrying."

"I wish I could," said Ken. "The guy's a psycho. In some sick way, he loves her. He's obsessed with her, and he'll do anything to get her back. He's obviously rich. If he's bribing the cops, they could lead him straight here, and then what? Even if some of the police are on our side, they might not find him until it's too late. Chopper will just show up here one night. He'll just show up and—"

"Stop *worrying!*" Trish pounded the table, making him jump. "If he finds us, there's nothing we can do about it anyway, so what's the point of freaking out?"

"Because he could *kill* us," snapped Ken. "What's the point of just waiting to die? You know, I'm starting to think we should leave the city. We should just go and never come back."

"Go where?"

"Anywhere! It's either that, or..."

"Or...?" Trish raised an eyebrow.

"Or maybe we could track him down on our own." Trish looked at him like he was crazy, but he seemed enthusiastic. "Yumi?" he called. She peeked up from her plate. "Where did you use to live? Like, do you remember where you were...you know...chained up?"

Yumi immediately shook her head.

"Eh?" Ken grunted, confused. "You mean you don't know, or you don't remember?"

She just shrugged.

"It doesn't matter," said Trish. "She was probably locked up alone, far away from other people, so no one could hear her yell for help. Besides, when she finally escaped, I doubt she was concerned with the address, if there even was one. For all we know, she was kept in a trailer or something."

Yumi nodded at Trish, finally confirming one of her longwinded theories.

"Is that true?" asked Ken. "He locked you in a trailer by yourself?"

She nodded again, glumly glancing downward.

"Oh... Then I guess we can't find him that way. He would've just moved your trailer after you escaped, huh? If you don't mind me asking, though, how did you get away, anyway?"

Yumi grabbed her collar, then mimed ripping it apart. She repeated this motion.

"You broke your shock collar?" he guessed.

She hesitated, then shook her head.

"You didn't break it?"

She nodded, then raised her arms high and spread them wide, as if hugging a huge invisible ball. She hopped out of her chair to emphasize her actions, then covered one ear and roared.

Ken interpreted her puzzling actions. *Really big? One ear? Loud roar?*

"Chopper?" he guessed. Yumi applauded, then returned to her chair. "What about Chopper?"

She mimed ripping her collar off again, then waited.

"He destroyed your shock collar?" he asked, and she nodded. "*Chopper* freed you?"

Apparently tired of nodding, she gave him the thumbs up instead.

"Why would Chopper free you?"

Yumi exhaled, also tired of miming, but she couldn't communicate without resorting to more charades. She gripped her collar and convulsed in her chair, faking an agonized face. She tugged and tugged, and then she pretended to destroy her collar once again, before standing to run in place.

"I get it," said Trish. "The big guy couldn't stand to see you in pain, eh?"

Yumi jogged a short distance before grabbing her leg. Balancing on one foot, she gently raked her claws across her ankle, then hurriedly limped forward a few steps.

"The cuts on your leg," Ken said, recalling the night he found her bleeding in the alley. "I see. Chopper didn't mean to let you escape. After he broke your collar, you took off. He tried to grab you, but he only scratched your leg. That makes sense—but how did you outrun him if you were hurt?"

Yumi sat back down. With one hand, she zoomed her fist between the plates like a speedboat. With the other, she walked her fingers across the table, and then her fingers hobbled onto her fist. Together, they rocketed away.

"You jumped on a pod? You mean like yesterday? You've pulled that crazy stunt before?"

Yumi nodded and clapped one last time, then she proceeded to eat her now cold meal.

"What an amazing girl," Trish chuckled, also digging into her soggy pancakes.

"No wonder he couldn't find you," said Ken. "A pod could've carried you across the whole city. The scratches on your leg were fresh when I found you, too... So, you ran away that same night?"

She held up her palm, signaling, *"Please, no more questions!"*

"Hmph... You really are amazing," Ken said, finally eating as well.

He habitually prepared for the day, washing and dressing, although he had nowhere to be or go. He spent the rest of the morning and most of the afternoon peeking through the curtains, pacing through the house, and sighing. The only productive thing he did was call about the damages to their apartment. Even when he watched TV with Yumi, Ken sat where he could see through the front and back windows, and he viewed the streets more than the screen.

That night, alone on the couch closest to the exits, he hardly slept, listening for footsteps and looking for unmarked trucks. The constant patter of raindrops grated on his frayed nerves for the next few days. Trapped inside the house and his paranoid mind, monitoring news networks for any indication he could go home, Ken eventually devised some defensive measures.

"I'd love to get my hands on a gun," he said to Trish, zipping up his windbreaker, "but unless I steal one from the police, that's not going to happen. The only thing we can do is run and hide."

"Hmph," Yumi confidently snorted, as if to say, *"Running is not our only option!"*

She pointedly flashed her claws, baring her teeth within the shade of her hooded sweater.

"You almost died the last time you fought," said Ken. "And you never would've stood a chance without going berserk. Even if you kill Chopper, your fever might kill you, and that's if you survive another heart attack. If it comes down to it, I know you'll protect me, but I don't want you to fight."

He affectionately mussed her hair, and she pouted, despite understanding.

"We need to be ready to run at all times, including when we're asleep. We'll move the bed into the living room when we get back," he told Trish. "Keep the alarm armed, even though it's light out, and if you go to the bathroom, keep the door open. And put on some shoes, okay?"

"If it'll make you feel better," she said grudgingly. "Where are you going, anyway?"

"I can't say. This way, you won't be able to tell anyone where we are."

"You're pretty serious about this, huh?"

"I'll see you soon, okay?" Ken hugged her goodbye.

She coughed uncontrollably.

"W-why are you wearing so much *perfume*?" she asked, swatting the air and backing away.

"If we're going outside, we should try to cover our scents."

"Go, then!" she said, pushing him toward the door. "You're stinking up the house!"

Using Trish's car, Ken drove downtown with Yumi. The weather finally simmered down to a gentle drizzle, so drivers and pedestrians populated the flooded streets and sidewalks. Every rolling tire and shuffling footstep caused ripples and splashes, but umbrellas weren't necessary.

On the way to their destination, they took long detours, cut through alleys, backtracked, and drove in circles, muddling their trail. If Trish's theories were correct, and Chopper tracked them from inside a truck, the creature's task would be doubly difficult if they spread their scents far and wide. They drove slowly with the windows rolled down through suburban areas. Ken doused some houses with the perfume he wore, and at stoplights, he covertly sprayed cars through his window. Finally, over three hours after they departed, they arrived at the shopping mall downtown.

Once inside, they separated. Ken emptied the perfume bottle into a potted plant, while Yumi rode the current of the crowd. With her hood hiding her ears, her baggy clothing concealing her tail, and her pockets covering her claws, she appeared completely human. If by some horrible coincidence The Breeder or one of his mods were at that mall, they would have never picked or sniffed her out of the pack. After Ken ditched and replaced his fragrant outfit at a skate shop, he joined Yumi at the wall of colognes and perfumes inside a nearby drugstore.

He glanced up at the daunting amount of choices.

"So, should we pick for ourselves or for each other?"

She poked him, then herself, then herself and him, and started sampling colognes.

"For each other, then," he said, plucking a feminine bottle off the shelf. He sprayed the air and sniffed the mist, but the sour citrus blend didn't suit her at all. He tried putting her traits into words. *Strong. Spirited. Free.* She was fierce yet comforting, honest yet mysterious, and the more Ken thought about her, the more she reminded him of the ocean. She was crashing waves and rippling water. She was soft sunlight and enduring stones. Once he knew what he wanted, he quickly found it: a soothing scent, deep and pungent, but sweet and spicy.

She had already chosen his new scent. When he gave it a whiff, it seemed weak and plain, but with her keen senses, she must have found some calming or exciting notes underneath. Whatever she liked about it, he never knew, but when she snuggled into him that night, snuffling his chest and neck, he couldn't have cared less about his cologne.

Although the only bed rested squarely in the middle of her living room, Trish slept on a couch by herself, far away from their choking saccharine fumes. Yumi lay on top of Ken, licking his face. He sank into the mattress beneath her warm body, as her tongue washed away his fears, but when she tenderly kissed his lips, his penis twitched, and he involuntarily turned his head. She pecked his cheek instead, but he gripped her shoulders and pushed her mouth away, pressing his hips into the bed so his cock couldn't reach her. It flexed anyway, tapping her crotch. He hurriedly twisted out from under her and sat up against the headboard. Ken couldn't see her face in the dark, though he could vividly envision her perplexed pout.

"Sorry, puppy, but my sister's *right there*," he whispered. "Could we maybe get some sleep?"

After they settled back beneath the blankets, Yumi spooned him, rubbing his chest with her pads and stroking her thumb across his belly like a guitar. Ken couldn't sleep, concerned that she might reach lower and fondle his balls.

Two days later, the local evening news finally reported on The Breeder.

"Trish! Yumi!" Ken called from the living room. "Come quick! I think they got him!"

The three of them huddled on the bed around the television. On the screen, a pretty reporter holding an umbrella and a microphone puddled through the parking lot at À La Mod.

"...And behind me, you can see some of the damages the war mod caused during its rampage," she said, motioning to the plastic sheet that prevented rain from entering the broken window.

"They sure are taking their sweet time fixing the place," said Trish.

"Police finally identified and apprehended the mod's owner last night," said the reporter.

"Yes!" Ken cheered, hugging Yumi and ruffling her hair.

"However, they still haven't found the bloodhound itself. The owner, who wishes to remain anonymous, says the mod attacked him and escaped a few weeks ago. It is on the loose, so be on the lookout. War mods are extremely dangerous, so if you see one, contact the authorities immediately. Do not approach it under any circumstances."

"What the hell?" Ken said, glancing at the window. "Chopper's still out there somewhere?"

"The owner accepted full responsibility for the damages, which include several vehicles and some of the slaves here at À La Mod. Police are also investigating reports that the war mod vandalized a nearby apartment building. Now, the owner won't serve any jail time under the condition that they reimburse all parties involved, but depending on how much damage the bloodhound actually caused, that could be one steep restaurant bill."

She signed off. The following story covered the recent flooding.

"What the fuck!?" Ken roared, practically jumping off the bed. "They barely even mentioned the break-in! Vandalized an apartment? What the hell is that? What about all the shit he did to Yumi? He attacked us! They fucking *caught* the bastard, and he's already out?"

"I guess he really could buy his way out of trouble," said Trish.

"This isn't right," Ken said, pacing. "He's free. Both those monsters, they're free."

Yumi bit her bottom lip and hugged her knees, pensive.

"If the police told them we're here..." he muttered. "If they know we're here..."

"Everybody just calm down, all right?" said Trish. "We'll figure something out."

"We have to go," he stated. "We can't live here anymore, and neither can you."

"Why the hell not? He's not after me, right?"

"What if he hurts you to get to Yumi, huh? What if he takes you hostage? This guy's insane, Trish. Are you just going to wait here for him to kidnap you, or kill you, or worse?"

"Well, where can we go?" she asked, looking atypically timid. "We don't know anyone outside the city we could stay with, and we can't just move. I'd have to sell my house, and you're in debt."

"I've been looking into some cheap spots where we could hide out, and there's a little place where we can rent a cabin," Ken said, petting Yumi. She stared at the floor. "It's not as far away as I'd like, but if we pack fast, we can leave before dark. We'll just have to figure out the rest from there..."

CHAPTER SIX

"I'm not your pet."

Although the rain stopped streaking from the cloudy orange sky, Trish's windshield wipers worked rapidly. Every time another car passed close, brown water smeared the glass. She couldn't distinguish lanes beneath the virtual swamp, but barricades along the perimeter highway orientated her enough that she could creep forward. Yumi huddled in the backseat with the stacks of luggage, food, and supplies that wouldn't fit in the trunk, so Trish couldn't see out of her back window. In the passenger's seat, Ken helped his sister find their way using the GPS on his phone.

"I can't see a damn thing," said Trish. "I don't know where the hell I'm going."

"We came here last year," said Ken. "It's by that amusement park. Just keep going."

Gradually, like a steel sunrise, the seasonal carnival rose over the horizon. Yumi leaned into the front seat, ogling the towering thrill rides, colourful game stalls, and compact roller coasters. Her cute smile compelled Ken to touch her, so he scratched under her chin and patted her head.

"I'll have to take you to a fair someday," he said, "after this is all over."

Trish turned off the highway toward a timbered area. Without the barricades, she straddled the ditches with only the treelines to indicate the flooded roads, but with some directions from Ken, they safely reached the wooded campgrounds. Yumi smelled pine through the air conditioning. With the luggage blocking her doors, she eagerly crawled over Ken's lap to escape. She frolicked through the parking lot. Her sandals flopped off, and she spun under the trees, reveling in nature, giggling.

It's the beach all over again, Ken thought, climbing out of the car.

"Come on, Yumi! You're gonna step on a pine cone or something!"

She picked up her sandals and jogged back to him, tongue lolling from her mouth. The gloomy weather meant only a couple avid fishermen occupied the site, so Ken could choose whichever cabin he liked. With security in mind, he chose one beside the lake that had plentiful windows and only one road in or out. Chopper likely wouldn't approach from the water, and the single entrance would make any approaching vehicles obvious, especially once Ken set up the motion sensor alarms he bought at the mall. According to their boxes, the alarms would "Prevent even your most rebellious mods from sneaking out," and it was a "Safe alternative to collars and cages." Judging by the image of a floppy-eared little girl, Ken assumed owners used them to train puppies, but they suited his needs just fine.

While Ken and Trish unpacked the car, Yumi jogged outdoors. While they sorted their clothes, she climbed trees. While they stocked the refrigerator, she watched the scarlet sunset. Ken called her into the cabin multiple times, but she refused to listen, preferring to amble about like a bunny.

"You can help, you know," he would argue. "You're spreading your scent!" he warned, but she ignored him, and by the time he finished unpacking, she had wandered into the dark woods, barely visible through the shrubs and branches.

"Yumi!" he called from the porch. She didn't respond. He cupped his mouth for extra volume. "Yuuumiii—!"

"Would you stop it?" Trish said, joining him outside. "You can't just lock her in a wooden box. I thought you bought her so she could be free."

"Yes, but I want her to be *safe*."

"Are you her boyfriend or her dad?" she asked. He didn't reply. "Let her have some fun."

"What's so fun about running around in the woods? I swear, she's more dog than human."

"Well, you've definitely been treating her that way lately."

"What? No, I haven't. What are you talking about?"

"You just don't seem as close as you were at the beach. I can't remember the last time I saw you two kiss. And that scratching her chin stuff in the car? What the hell was that? I mean, you cuddle sometimes, and you sleep together, but so do we."

"We don't *sleep* together. Then again, I haven't really slept with her in a while, either."

"*Oooh*," Trish cooed, leaning over his shoulder. "So, you screwed the pooch, eh?"

"It was one time," Ken said, brushing her off.

"Well, don't leave me hanging! Give me the details."

"There's nothing to say, really. It was...nice, but ever since that night, I just..."

"You just...?" Trish raised an eyebrow.

"Nothing," he said, heading back inside. "It's nothing. Can we just drop it?"

"Sure, whatever," she said, following him indoors.

The quaint cabin consisted of one spacious room complete with a kitchen, with one functional bathroom and one cramped bedroom. It included electricity and plumbing, but no television, though other cabins possessed fewer luxuries. If funds ran low, he could always downgrade to granola bars and outhouses, but he intended to find more permanent lodgings before that happened.

That night, Yumi returned dripping in her underwear, clutching her muddy clothes. Ken and Trish stared at her from one of the two facing sofas. She tossed her squishy lump of clothing in the corner, padded into the space between the couches, and vigorously *shook* her body dry, splattering Ken and Trish. She giggled, as they spluttered and protested, and then she plopped herself face down on the opposing sofa, flattening her bare breasts on the cushions, as though she was sunbathing.

"There's something wrong with you," Ken said, wiping water off his face. "It's not even raining. Did you jump in the lake?"

Yumi sleepily nodded.

"If you have any ticks, it's your own fault. I'm not taking them off for you."

She shrugged and turned her back on him, curling up to nap. He thought he saw her grin.

"More dog than human," he mumbled. "I swear..."

Trish just laughed.

At first, Ken found Yumi's frivolous behaviour charming. Her irrepressible spirit and untamed attitude inspired and enticed him from the start, but when her actions endangered their lives, they became less endearing and more infuriating. Despite his best efforts, he couldn't control or contain Yumi. She spent most of the next three days in the forest and the lake, returning to the cabin only to eat, sleep, and occasionally snuggle. He persistently warned her, but she refused to listen or relent.

"Did you forget why we're here?" he scolded her one blustery day. She sat cross-legged on a large rock in torn denim shorts and a frayed T-shirt. "Chopper's going to get your scent. The wind is blowing *toward* the city, and you're not even wearing your perfume. Do you want them to find us?"

She rolled her eyes.

"I get it," he said. "You wanna be *free* and feel the wind in your hair and all that shit, but there are more important things to worry about right now—like your *life*. Enough is enough already. Now, come back inside."

She scoffed, gazing across the choppy lake.

"Stop being selfish! You're not the only one in danger, you know. What if something happens to my sister because you're off chasing the fucking *squirrels*? You're acting like a mindless animal."

Yumi glowered at him with an anger he hadn't seen since she bit his arm.

"You can be pissed all you want," said Ken. "Just get inside. Get inside *now*, Yumi!"

As expected, she defiantly bounded off the rock and darted into the woods.

"Get back here, Yumi!" he pointlessly cried, as she shrank between the trees. "YUMI!"

She vanished within the forest. Ken trudged back to the cabin, storming inside and slamming the door so hard the logs almost splintered. Trish glanced up from her tablet and paused whichever noisy movie she was streaming.

"Trouble in rainy, miserable paradise?" she asked, setting the device beside her on the sofa.

"She's out of her mind," he said, slouching onto the other couch. "I don't understand. It's like she wants to get caught."

"I doubt that," she said, standing up. "She just hates being...trapped. From what I've seen, she doesn't even like wearing clothes. With all this nature around, how can you expect her to sit still?"

"It's just frustrating," he grumbled, burying his face in his hands. "She's feeling less and less like my girlfriend and more like my *bitchy* teenage daughter."

"Maybe that's for the best," Trish said, stretching as she approached Ken.

"What do you mean by that?"

"Well..." She heavily dropped onto the cushion beside Ken. The sofa sagged under her weight, and he involuntarily leaned against her shoulder. "If you don't feel as strongly about her anymore, maybe you should let her know. No one's forcing you to make out with your mod. Look after her, care about her, protect her, but if the passion's gone, maybe it's time to move on with someone else."

"Like who?"

Trish nudged Ken. "Who do you think, stupid?"

He finally took an intimate look at Trish. She wore her version of pajamas, a loose tank top that exposed the tops and sides of her hefty boobs, and short cotton shorts that bared her smooth legs. What little fabric she wore clung to her moist, curvaceous body, and she smelled like strawberry shampoo. She brushed a spiral of orange hair away from her twinkling emerald eyes and simpered slightly. Ken had never seen her look so cute. He diverted his gaze and gulped, and his cheeks tingled.

"This might seem out of nowhere, but I've always kinda liked you, even when we were kids," she said, swaying side to side, bumping his arm. "I just figured you only ever saw me as your big sister, so I never said anything. I didn't wanna make things weird between us, you know?"

"Yeah," he said. "I mean, I get it. It's not like I've never...looked at you that way."

"Right?" she smiled, leaning on his thigh. Her warm hand squeezed. "We've been through so much together over the years. It's only natural that we'd develop feelings for each other, right?"

"Right," he carefully replied. "I mean, I've thought about us. I've thought about...you."

"And? What do you think about me, Ken?"

"Well, I look up to you," he said dully. "I care about you, even though I don't always show it. You always look out for me and support me, even now. You're the reason I'm alive today, and..."

"That's sweet, but that's not what I meant," she laughed. "I meant, how do you *feel* about me?" She shuffled closer. "Not as your big sister." Her breathy words tickled his neck. "As a *woman*."

"I wish I could tell you." He swallowed. "I'm still not sure."

"Well, maybe this'll help you decide," Trish said, then she grabbed his head, cranked his face toward her, and reeled him in for a kiss. Dozens of impulses triggered inside his brain: *Fight her off. Kiss her now. Shove her away. Pull her close. Struggle. Indulge. Break her heart. Taste her mouth. Push. Embrace.* He decided too late. She kissed him hard, inhaling deeply through her nose. In the moment, he melted. Her soft lips tasted of cherry lip gloss, and her fiery hair brushed his cheeks. Ken grasped her hips and crept up her sides. He tucked his hands under her round breasts, and they drooped over his thumbs, and once he finally found a solid grip, he *pushed* against her ribs.

She resisted, panting. Their lips parted, so she absurdly thrust her tongue forward. He pushed again, hard. She sprawled backward, spreading her legs, expecting him to climb on her, but he stared down on her, motionless. Humiliation painted her face red, and she scrambled upright, indignant.

"What the hell, Ken?" she spat. "Are we doing this or not?"

"Sorry," he said coolly, "but I'm with Yumi."

"Then break up with her first. I've waited years for you; I can wait a few more hours."

"I'm not going to betray her like that just so I can fool around with my sister—"

"I'm not your sister!" Trish screeched, making him flinch. "I don't get it. You'll fuck your pet, but I'm not good enough for you?"

"It's not a competition."

"Yes, it is," she argued. "Come on, I wanna know. What do you see in her, huh? You've known this girl for like a month. She's brought you nothing but trouble. She can't even hold a conversation. Besides a fucking *tail*, what does she have that I don't?"

"Nothing, I guess."

"Is it because she's hot?" asked Trish. "Is that it? Is it because she's tall and skinny and pretty, and I'm just your fat ugly sister?"

"You're not fat," Ken said, unsure how to reply, "or ugly. You're really cute, actually."

"Then what's the problem? I think you're cute. I like you. What's wrong with me?"

Trish wiped her shiny eyes before her tears dripped. Ken consolingly touched her soft thigh, but she smacked his hand off.

"You wanna know what I think?" she asked spitefully.

"Not really," he said apprehensively.

"I think you were lonely," she said anyway. "I think you stumbled on this hot, vulnerable girl, and you thought that if you rescued her, she'd be so grateful she'd just fall into your lap. And she did. And now you regret it."

Ken contemplated her words and let her vent.

"If you hadn't bought a slave, we wouldn't be living here in a shack scared for our lives. We'd be safe at home, drinking wine. Maybe we could've gone to the beach more often, and on rainy days, we could've stayed in and cuddled. If it wasn't for her, maybe we'd be something more by now."

"It's not her fault we're not together, Trish."

"Deep down, I know that," she sniffed, "but I can't help but wonder."

"Sounds like you're the one with regrets."

"Maybe," she laughed sadly. "I definitely regret pouring my heart out to you like this."

"Well, I don't," he said, grasping her hand. She didn't smack him this time. "You know, we can still stay in and cuddle. And maybe we could drive into the city and pick up a bottle of something."

"Are you sure? Wouldn't you be *betraying* Yumi?"

"Why? I'm not allowed to cuddle with my sister? *Ooph—!*"

Trish punched him in the gut. He sharply poked and tickled her in retaliation, and they locked hands, playfully and painfully twisting each other's fingers. They grappled awkwardly at first, aware of every pinch and graze, wary of what they touched, but soon they tumbled and giggled on the couch like roughhousing kids. After several minutes of wrestling, Ken lay on Trish, listening to her heartbeat through her sweaty breasts. She curled her legs around him and combed his hair with her nails.

"This isn't enough," she breathed. "It's just making it worse."

"We're pushing it as it is," he said, sinking into her squishy body. Her warm skin soothed him, and he thought, *I'm glad you're kinda chubby.* Temptation attacked him; he nearly pecked her neck. Supressing the urge to burrow his face into her cleavage, he said, "Take it or leave it."

"Fine," she exhaled, rubbing his back. "I guess this is good enough—for now."

Suddenly the shrill shrieks of an alarm sliced through the cabin's cracks. Startled, Ken hopped off Trish and dashed to the window. Alone, Yumi covered her ears and pouted, approaching the door.

"False alarm," he told Trish. "It's just Yumi." She released a relieved sigh.

Alarm still blaring behind her, Yumi entered the cabin with her tail tucked between her legs. She stood near the door and waited until the electronic squeals subsided, then she coyly neared Ken. Fiddling with her fingernails, she pinned back her ears and lowered her eyes. Ken accepted her with open arms, but she clutched her hands to her chest, and rather than embrace him, she steadily walked forward until they bumped foreheads. Her tongue flicked his face.

"No, I'm the one who should be sorry," he said tenderly. He hugged her waist and tugged her close. "I've just been so worried about you. I barely see you anymore. I feel like I might lose you..."

"Um..." Trish peeped, rising from the couch. "I think I'll just, uh, make a quick shopping run, maybe do some laundry. Can you disable the alarms while I change?"

"Sure," Ken replied, reluctantly releasing Yumi. She waited inside while he switched off the motion sensors, and once Trish drove away, he reset the alarms and jogged back into the cabin. Yumi sat on the sofa, staring at the floorboards, nibbling her lip, and rubbing her hands together.

"I wish you could tell me what you're thinking," he said, joining her on the couch. The cushions still contained Trish's latent heat. "It might be annoying, but can I ask you some yes or no questions?"

She hesitated, then nodded.

"All right... Well, I should probably get this out of the way first," he said, taking a deep breath. "Trish, uh... kissed me earlier."

Yumi leered at him, and her ears perked up. The room, and his clothes, felt sticky and humid.

"I turned her down, but we sort of...*cuddled* afterward. I'm wondering if that's okay. I mean, she'd like it if we cuddled every now and then. No kissing or anything, just...you know. Petting."

Ken expected her to immediately shake her head. Surprisingly, she immediately nodded.

"Really?" he asked skeptically. "What if I, uh...lay on her chest like a pillow?"

Yumi shrugged and nodded simultaneously, basically telling him, "*I don't care.*"

"Hmph... Good to know. Thanks for understanding, I guess. Anyway, onto my other questions. How much do you like it out here?" he asked, though that wasn't a yes or no question. "Er, I mean, would you like to live someplace like this? I was thinking about where we should move, and—"

She cut him off, nodding so vigorously he worried for her vertebrae.

"All right. I'll keep that in mind. Now, next question." He paused, piling weight on his words. "I feel like you've been really distant lately. Have you stopped trying to hide from...you-know-who? Have you given up?"

Yumi considered the question for a few seconds, then nodded.

Ken furrowed his brow. "But why?" he wondered. "Why make it easier for him to find you?"

She shrugged, unable to respond any other way.

"Please, help me understand. Even if you're bored, is it worth going outside if you get caught? Why take that risk? Do you *want* him to catch you?"

He had asked that somewhat rhetorically, yet she glanced downward and somberly nodded.

"W-what?" he gasped. "Why? That doesn't make sense. Why would you want to go back?"

She held up four fingers on one hand and poked his chest with the other.

"Four?" he guessed. "Four...you? For me? You'd go back for me?"

She nodded again, and tears blossomed on her eyes, and he realized why she distanced herself from him, and wandered alone in the forest for hours, and so leniently shared him with Trish.

"I see... You're trying and give yourself up, s-so I won't get hurt," he asked, unable to supress the tremors in his voice. "Is that what you think? Y-you think I'd be better off without you?"

She nodded once more, shaking her tears loose like fruit off a branch.

"Oh, *Yumi*," he said, pinning her arms to her sides with his snug embrace. She shuddered so hard, she almost broke his grip. "You don't have to sacrifice yourself for me. You don't have to suffer through this alone. Whatever happens, we'll face this together. You and me, right, puppy?"

She hugged him tightly, clutching the muscles in his back, and tackled him into the cushions. Like that, she quietly wept, squeaking and sniffling occasionally. His chest ached beneath the crushing weight of her audible anguish, though the weight of her furry body helped alleviate his heartache.

"It's okay, puppy," he said, stroking the fuzz near her spine. "You're not alone..."

Yumi kissed his neck, and her wet nose tapped his earlobe. Ken inhaled her scent, an earthy blend of fresh pine and sweat that suited her rugged, wiry physique. She leaned backward. Her eyes glistened, and she smiled faintly, before taking his face in her hands and bending low until their lips and noses touched. Lust and affection stewed together with something that tasted like shame.

Yumi sat up and straddled him, gripped the bottom of her tattered shirt, and slowly peeled it off. She tossed the cloth aside and rubbed herself from her neck to her breasts, lingering on a nipple. Ken gulped and looked away, but she grabbed his chin and forced him to look at her, and she kissed him again just like that, sliding her slimy tongue into his mouth. His heart pounded, and he tingled all over, and his cock bulged against her crotch. He twisted his hips. She misread his wriggling and stood off of him, presenting her ass, and then she gradually pulled down her shorts and panties, unveiling her round, bare bottom. Ken unenthusiastically removed his own shirt, as if he was about to bathe.

After stripping, Yumi hungrily removed his pants for him, as he rubbed his eyes. Something hot and slippery absorbed his dick, and he heard sloppy slurping. He stared at the ceiling for a couple minutes, and then she crawled on top of him, wagging her long tongue. She reached back. He watched her grasp his now stiff, twitching cock and sit on it. All at once, he stabbed up through her wet tube, and pleasure and guilt stabbed his brainstem. He writhed, and she bounced.

She moaned, and he heard chains rattle. She slammed her pussy down onto his penis, and he saw the steel hound. A delightful sting shot through his body, and visions of torture zapped his mind. He felt himself soften, despite her strong, steady stream of stimulation. Remorse and anger brewed inside him like thundering black clouds, and he abruptly heaved Yumi off of him and swung his legs over the edge of the couch. In her frenzy, she swiftly moved around to sit on his lap, but he gripped her hips and thrust her on the cushion beside him, then he cried out, "Enough, Yumi! *Stop!*"

She gawked at him, bewildered. He buried his face in his hands and glared down at his slick, shrinking cock.

"I've had enough," he said, panting. "I can't. I'm sorry, Yumi, but I just can't..."

She concernedly placed a paw on his shoulder. He accepted her touch, but he didn't budge.

"I'm sorry," he repeated. "I can't stop thinking about it. Every time I touch you... Every time we kiss or get close, I think of everything that *bastard* did to you, and I can't do it." He pulled his head out of his hands, revealing his red eyes. Yumi bit her lip, also resisting tears. "How can you still want to...after all that? Do you even want to? Or do you just feel pressured to do it, like that's what you're supposed to do?"

Yumi removed her hand to wipe her leaking face, and he stroked her scruffy head.

"If you really want to...have sex," he said, with some difficulty, "I'll try to get over your past. But I want you to be sure, okay?"

She nodded sullenly. He kissed her cheek, and then she got up to get dressed.

"I'm sorry, Yumi," he said again, picking his clothes off the floor. For some reason, he recalled that Trish once told him mods only do what they're trained to do. "We'll try again tomorrow, maybe."

To the startling fanfare of the puppy training alarms, Trish returned around sunset with clean laundry, armfuls of groceries, and one huge brown bag. She unpacked the brown bag first, removing six bottles of wine—one red and one white for each person. Trish finished off her red within an hour, not so subtly claiming, "Nothing cures heartbreak like liquor," before drinking it from the bottle.

Ken and Yumi drank their first glasses with dinner— potato chips and hot dogs—though she drained her first bottle not long after Trish. He might have scolded her for chugging it, but he felt responsible for her dejected state, and at least she drank indoors.

Halfway through her white, Trish blatantly snuggled on the couch with Ken, without knowing that Yumi knew about their kiss. She caressed his chest and abs and rested against his shoulder. Yumi lounged on the opposite sofa, spying, and she didn't seem to care, until Trish boldly pecked his neck. She immediately marched over and sat sideways on Ken's lap, hugging his head and nuzzling his face, with her back turned to the other woman.

"Marking your territory, huh?" Trish scoffed, rising to pour herself another glass. "That's fine. I'll just have to steal your spot the next time you go outside to piss."

Yumi growled over her shoulder.

"Easy, ladies," said Ken. "I'm really not worth fighting over. Can't we just share?" he joked.

"Sorry, Ken," Trish said, dumping her remaining wine into a water glass. She paused to gulp down a mouthful. "I'd have to be drunker than this to have a threesome with the family dog."

Yumi launched off his lap at Trish, baring her teeth and seething.

"What're you gonna do, huh?" Trish asked, stepping up to Yumi. They butted heads, and their eyebrows clashed like duelling caterpillars. "You're all bark, little girl. I'll put you to sleep."

"Stop it, Trish!" Ken said, rushing between the two women. "Why are you being a bitch?"

"Oh, *I'm* the bitch?" she laughed. "Are you sure you know what that word means?"

"Enough fighting," he said, gently separating the women. Yumi allowed him to push her back, but Trish knocked his arm away. "This is my fault, anyway... Yumi." He faced her first. "I was wrong. I can make excuses, but I shouldn't have kissed Trish. I should've pushed her off sooner, and I'm sorry. And Trish." He faced her next, and she scowled back. "I'm sorry, too. I never should've..." he hesitated, searching for the right pacifying words, but she finished his sentence. "*I never should've—*"

"Bought that whore?"

Ken and Yumi glared at Trish, and something frightening must have flared inside their eyes, because she backed up against the counter and swallowed the rest of her wine.

"What'd you just call her?" he asked, glancing back at Yumi. Her taut lips portrayed her rage, and her fingers curled into sharp hooks, but her shiny eyes swam with tears.

"You heard me," said Trish. "It's like I told you before. She's brought us nothing but trouble. Without this whore in our lives, everything would be perfect..."

Yumi lunged—for the door. She burst into the darkness, leaving only a few teardrops on the floor and the echoes of her sobs in the air. Ken chased her outside, but she already disappeared. The clouds blotted out the moonlight, and the howling wind overpowered the sound of harried footsteps on fallen leaves.

"Yumi!" he cried. Only the wind replied. "Yuuumiii!"

When he stormed into the cabin minutes later, he found Trish leaning against the refrigerator, nursing her third bottle. As she went for another swig, he stomped over and smacked the bottle out of her hand. It shattered against the floor, as he grabbed her shirt and pressed her against the fridge.

"Hey, not so rough!" she yelled. "Should we move this to the bedroom?"

"Shut up!" he snarled. "Do you even realize what you might've done? Do you have any idea?"

"What? She'll come crawling back. She always comes back."

"Yeah? And what if she doesn't this time?"

"Then I guess it wasn't meant to be," she chuckled.

Ken gripped her bushy hair and knocked her bobbling head against the freezer door.

"You wanna know why she wanders through the woods by herself?" he asked. "Huh?"

"Because she's bored?"

"No," he rasped. "It's to protect *us*. She wants them to catch her alone. She feels so worthless, she'd rather hand herself over to the bastard who *raped* her than risk our lives anymore. But what do you do? You call her a whore. You bully her until she cries, and do you even fucking care?"

"I care," she claimed. "I mean, I don't want anything bad to happen to her, I just..."

"You just what, Trish? You just want her gone so you don't have to share? You've never given a damn about Yumi. You just play nice so she won't be suspicious, but she knows what you really are now, and so do I. To you, she might be just a dog," he said, "but you're a fucking *snake*—"

Trish whacked him, and his ear rang like a flash grenade popped.

"So what? At least I'm not a goddamn *mutt*," she slurred. "Those things took everything from us—our parents, childhood—but I've done everything for you! I raised you. I saved you. I protected you when no one else would. You'd be dead without me, and you'd still rather fuck that monster?"

"I'm not your pet," Ken said, wiping blood off his lip. "I'm grateful for you taking care of me, even now, but you don't own me. I belong to someone else."

Furious noises crackled from her throat, as she struggled for a response. Ken reached into her purse on the countertop. Before she could react, he fished out her keys and hurried to the front door, jingling.

"Hey!" said Trish. "Where do you think you're going?"

"Where do you think?" he said, shoving the door aside. "I'm going to find Yumi."

Trish stumbled onto the porch, as he ignited her car's engine.

"So, you're just gonna steal my car, just like that?" she screamed. "You can't leave me here! What if that bloodhound shows up? How will I get away, huh?"

"I'd rather leave you here than leave her out there," he told her, "but if you're not too petty, you can always come along and help."

Trish paced the porch, hands on her hips, grinding her teeth. Soon, her concern trumped her animosity toward Yumi, and after giving an agitated groan, she squeezed into the car beside Ken. He drove off, tripping the training alarms, and she covered her ears, as the trees seemingly squealed.

Ken slowly circled the retreat for roughly half an hour, calling out his window for Yumi. If she resided on the campsite, she surely heard him, but she either ignored him or avoided his passenger's boisterous voice. Trish begrudgingly shouted her name, mixing in half-hearted apologies.

"Sorry we made out!" she belted out her window. "Come on, Yumi, I said I'm sorry already!"

Ken eventually drove off the campsite, traversing muddy paths to the highway before turning back. Carnival lights twinkled over the horizon like red and blue stars, and he faintly heard childish tunes. He pictured Yumi and the goofy grin she wore whenever she glimpsed that fair, but when he imagined her weeping alone in the dark forest, his eyes stung and blurred. Trish nodded off after two hours of fruitless searching. Ken returned to the cabin hoping to find Yumi snoozing in the bedroom, but he found only flat sheets and cold pillows. Despite falling asleep in the car, Trish stayed awake watching movies on her tablet and sipping wine on the couch. Ken lay awake waiting for Yumi in bed, listening for activity from the front door, but he passed out after a few anxiety-ridden hours.

Ken woke after noon to the sound of Trish snoring through the open bedroom door. Sunlight streaked through his windows. He stirred, grasping across the blankets, and his heart sank when he realized he was all alone. Something sharp and bright suddenly blinded him, but when he closed his eyes, the pain subsided. He tentatively opened them again and noticed a shiny object by his bedside. Dodging the sunbeam reflecting off of it, he focused his bleary vision on the item, and he gasped.

Yumi's collar glinted on the nightstand.

CHAPTER SEVEN

"One adult and one mod."

Ken tore off his blankets, grabbed Yumi's glimmering collar off the nightstand, and leaped out of bed. He scanned the kitchen and living room. Empty wine bottles cluttered the countertops, and Trish slumbered on a couch in her street clothes. He smelled the fruity fumes wafting off her, but the scent of soap lured him into the bathroom. Ragged denim littered the floor, droplets pooled in the bathtub, and humid warmth clung to the air.

"She was here," he murmured, racing outside. He spotted a dewy spider web on the porch. A tepid breeze rattled the trees, and the campgrounds stirred with chirping birds and shadows, but no mods. "She was *just* here," he repeated in frustration, ducking back inside to fetch the car keys. After scooping them up, he habitually sought his mobile phone before he left. He checked the counters, the nightstand, and the pockets of the jeans he wore yesterday, but he couldn't find it. Combing the cabin, he noticed that Trish was sleeping on her tablet, but rather than rip it out from under her breasts like a tablecloth, he used the cabin's landline to call his phone.

He listened for his ringtone, or perhaps the quiet buzz of the vibration, but silence reigned. However, someone answered his call.

"Ken?" asked Yumi.

His heart skipped in the best way. "Yumi? Where are you? Why'd you take my phone?"

She didn't respond, but he heard chatter and chimes in the background. He swiftly hung up, washed and dressed for the day, and woke Trish.

"*Trish*," he whispered loudly, shaking her shoulder. "Trish!"

"Bwuh?" She stretched awake, fussing and yawning.

"I'm heading out," he said clearly. "Don't freak out when you hear the alarms, okay? Of course, if you hear them again, call me right away."

"Whatever..." she mumbled.

He left her to rehydrate and recover, then excitedly drove away.

The sunny campground resembled a swampland. Ken plodded through the sodden landscape, evading the cavernous puddles and muddy patches that would slow or stop his progress. He sped off the grounds, through the woods, and on the highway. On the horizon, the amusement park ballooned before him, swelling from a multicolour jumble of steel into an impressive, extensive exhibition. Ken had lost track of time inside the cabin, but the astounding number of cars in the packed dirt parking lot told him it was probably the weekend. Parking far away from the festivities, he jogged to the gate, where he spotted Yumi.

She sat alone in the dirt like a beggar. Most passersby barely glanced at her, but a few men overtly ogled her as they passed. Ken wondered if they recognized her from online, though he found it difficult to dwell on her past when she looked so radiant today. Yumi peered about the lot like a teen belle awaiting a blind date, anxiously smoothing her baby blue sundress. She warily eyed strangers who ventured too close, grasping the bulges in her pockets, but when she smelled Ken, her anxiety fled her face, and she keenly bolted at him through the scattered crowd.

She bowled into him, and he almost toppled beneath her six-foot frame, but they settled into an intimate embrace. People rudely stared, but he couldn't have cared less what they thought of him and Yumi. He separated from her only to pull her thick leather collar out of his pants pocket.

"When I first saw this, I thought you were telling me goodbye," Ken said, displaying the band, "but it was the opposite, wasn't it? You wanted me to follow you, to get closer to you..."

Yumi nodded, twisting coyly.

"Thanks for luring me out of that hole," he said, raising her necklace. She turned her back to him, and he strapped the belt around her scars so the golden nameplate gleamed at her throat. In return, she emptied her pockets and gave him back his phone, playfully sticking out her tongue. "If you hadn't set this up, I might still be sitting in that cabin, living in fear," he said, tucking the device away. She fondly stroked her collar. "I got the fear part right, but I guess I forgot to live. Well, I'm done being afraid. I'll take the risk. From now on, I want to live with you. So, how about we get started?"

He extended his hand, and she happily clasped it, and they stepped up to the ticket booth.

"One adult and one mod," Ken told the vendor.

"Are you her owner?" the man asked.

He gazed sideways at Yumi. She jittered, grinning from ear to pointy ear.

"Yeah," he said proudly, showing his ownership license. "I'm hers..."

After receiving coloured wristbands from the vendor, they strolled on the grassy fairgrounds. Yumi clung to his arm like lint for a few steps, but then she urgently broke away from Ken, spinning at the noisy carnival games, gawking up at the daunting steel structures, and sniffing at the fried food stands. Unsurprisingly, she followed her nose to a stall that sold deep-fried, bacon-wrapped turkey legs. Ken chased her, but before he caught up, she shoved her way to the front of the line, despite the hail of insults from those she mercilessly cut. He pushed through the aggravated crowd, apologizing profusely, until he reached Yumi. She leaned into the stall, dreamily drooling on a cooling turkey leg.

"Hey!" the cook cried, shooing her away. "Is this your mutt?" he asked Ken.

"S-sorry, she's a little excited," he chuckled nervously. "We'll take *that* one." He pointed to the leg she slobbered on, promptly paid for it, and fled with the food (and Yumi) before the mob attacked.

Before they reached the seating area, she ravenously clawed at the turkey leg.

"Take it easy!" Ken said, raising it out of her reach. "Let's find somewhere to sit first."

She jumped, and with her hands dangling at her sides, she chomped into the leg. She hung there for half a second, like a fish flopping on a hook, and then ripped a mouthful of meat off the bone. She chewed cheerfully on the crispy chunk, salivating.

Ken gaped at the bite mark, then gazed around the crowded fair, blushing.

"What's the matter with you?" he scolded her, sternly waving the turkey in front of her face. "People are staring enough as it is. I'm hungry, too, but can't you wait until—?"

"*Grawr!*" she snarled cutely, biting the leg. Ken struggled to yank it out of her powerful jaws, and she growled and violently rattled her head. The heated tug-of-war bout began.

"Stop it, Yumi!" he shouted, gripping the bone. "That's too big a bite! You're gonna eat it all!"

She grabbed his shoulders and pushed off of him for more leverage. The tough layer of fried bacon tore between her teeth, and she peeled off a hunk of turkey the size of his fist. She cupped her hands under her messy mouth, which she couldn't even fully close, and cheekily smiled at Ken.

"So that's how you wanna play, huh?" he said, urgently eating the leg like an ear of corn. Yumi hurriedly gulped down her mouthful and chomped the leg again, and the two of them munched their meaty club right there, until nothing remained but a greasy, glistening bone.

Satisfied and somewhat embarrassed, they cleaned their oily faces and fingers with napkins and bottled water. Ken scanned the park for their next escapade, but his stomach churned at the mere sight of the roiling rides. He rubbed his belly, favoring the carnival games.

"I don't know how you're feeling," he said, "but I think I'd rather stay on the ground for now."

Yumi gratefully nodded, then belched, before Ken led her toward the nearest stall.

He didn't expect to win. He expected rigged games of chance and exceedingly difficult games of skill, but Ken wanted the full fair experience for Yumi, scams and all.

Coincidentally, she dominated games of strength. On her first throw at a stack of metal milk bottles, she whipped the ball with such force the air whistled and the steel *cracked* like thunder. The game's operator fussed over one bottle, believing she chipped it, but he awarded her a prize anyway. She picked out a huge, adorable stuffed animal—a husky puppy sticking out its pink felt tongue.

"You know, it sort of looks like you," Ken teased, "except it's way cuter. Maybe I should take her home instead..."

She punched his shoulder and then snuggled her fluffy new friend, nuzzling its plastic nose. He gave the oversized pup a piggyback ride, as she effortlessly won a few other games. She slung the rubber sledgehammer down on the pressure plate, sending the red light up to strike the virtual bell. She walloped the punching bag, scoring the maximum 999 points. However, she failed to catch even one goldfish, at least without cheating. Her stupid paper net shredded with every flick of her wrist, and her frustration mounted until she snatched a fish out of the shallow pool with her bare hands.

"Are you sure you're not actually a cat?" asked Ken. "Or maybe a bear?"

She smugly plopped the goldfish back into the water and then helped Ken carry her prizes to the parking lot. She reluctantly left her husky puppy in the hot car, pressing her forehead to the backseat window, but after Ken assured her no one would steal her toys, she toddled after him and took his hand. He pulled her back through the fairgrounds to the rides.

Despite weeks of anticipation, she couldn't disguise her trepidation. She regarded the short roller coasters like vipers, and she shrank before the giant wheel, clutching her hands to her chest.

"What's the matter?" asked Ken. "You rode a pod. Twice. On the *outside*. Compared to that, this is nothing."

Still, she shook her head and hugged herself. He almost chuckled at her atypical timidity.

"All right, then," he began, massaging her stiff shoulders. "Let's start with something small..."

He scanned the park for the mildest machine that might still provide them some pleasure. The spinning teacups appeared too tame, according to the bored expressions of some children on the ride, but he noticed how Yumi gawked at the whirling, dizzying scrambler. She moved her head in wobbly circles, as if attempting to follow a single car through the chaos. Ken pulled her to the queue, and five minutes later, they sat strapped to a steel chair suspended a few metres off the ground. Yumi chewed her lip, gripping the bar across her lap. He peeled her taut fingers off the metal and ran his thumb over her white knuckles. The ride jolted sideways, and her whole body stiffened.

"When you're scared, just look at me," said Ken, gazing into her eyes.

She gazed back, as the scrambler steadily sped up. The background blurred behind him, and her teeth slipped off her lip. Delight swopped through her stomach, and she smiled. G-forces pressed her against Ken, and she laughed, as the ride hit full velocity. The whirring machine and whipping wind couldn't muffle her shrieks. Like a giddy little girl, she giggled, high and light as a bell ringing in his ear. Ken chuckled at the pure elation on her face.

He almost cupped his ears after they boarded their first clunking roller coaster, she squealed so loud. The train dipped and shook them at bewildering speeds, slamming their hips together like billiard balls. Yumi squeaked and practically bounced in her chair, and her eyes flared like blue flames, and her tongue flapped out of her mouth like a pink flag. Ken stared at her beautiful smiles, even as he zipped and zoomed along the track, savouring the rare sight. He compared how often she laughed to how often she sobbed, then he removed one hand from the railing to caress her thigh.

As they whooshed around a corner, their chair tilted, and Yumi fell into Ken. She kissed him forcefully. He squeezed the tensed muscles in her leg. At the risk of banging teeth, they made a game of pecking whenever the car shoved them up together on the sharper turns. Sometimes they missed, smooching cheeks and chins. The woman in the car behind them glowered at their public display of affection, yet they kissed whenever possible, uninhibited, until the teal sky faded to dusky orange.

Although she rode roller coasters all evening, Yumi shrunk within the shadow of the giant, lethargic wheel spinning at the back of the fairgrounds. She followed a chair upward, as it leisurely drifted toward the clouds like a balloon. She clenched her teeth harder the higher it climbed, but her face steadily relaxed the closer the chair sank to the ground. Somebody suddenly grabbed her hand, and she flinched, but when she realized who snuck up on her, her features softened.

"What's wrong?" asked Ken. "Are you afraid of heights?"

She bashfully nodded.

"Hm... That's funny," he said playfully. "I thought we were done living in fear."

Yumi smirked at that, then she nodded decisively and tugged him to the boarding platform. Despite her initial zeal, she decelerated with every step toward the wheel. By the time they reached the queue, the previous passengers had already unloaded, and she cowered behind Ken like a knight guarding against a shower of arrows, but when half the sun dipped under the horizon, the wheel automatically flashed to life, and she peeked out from behind her shield. The spokes shone electric red and yellow, and pink and green bulbs reflected off her wide eyes. Enchanted and distracted, she forgot her fear and shuffled with Ken into an empty chair, but once their seat began to sway and rise, she frantically clung to him like a frightened child.

The wheel turned torturously slow, prolonging her terror. People shrank to skittering insects beneath her, and the colourful rows of game and food stalls transformed into bright candies. Even the scrambler and the roller coasters that once terrified her appeared as blinking children's toys. She panted, squeezing her eyes shut and gripping Ken's arm hard enough to leave fingerprints.

Ken smoothly stroked her hair. Her eyes flickered back open. He petted her tenderly, rubbing between her ears. She breathed peacefully. They returned to the ground, finishing their first rotation, and as they rose again, Yumi remained calm. She watched the many tiny people scurry like mice. She watched the other rides spin and rattle like tin toys. From fifty meters above the planet, she watched the tangerine sun sink onto the other side of the world. Releasing her crushing grip on

Ken, she gently embraced him instead. She nuzzled his shoulder and purred.

"Ken..." she spoke softly. Something warm dripped onto his arm. "You... M-me..."

He kissed her immediately. Another tear dripped down her face, trickling slowly through the faint fuzz. Her mouth stretched into a smile, so he kissed her rosy cheeks instead, erasing her tears with his lips. Hot pressure heaved within his chest like magma under a volcano. His heart and lungs ached, and relief only came once he spoke the words roiling through his restless soul.

"I love you, Yumi," he said, as they crossed the starry sky. "I love you so much, I'd even die for you. I'm tired of being afraid. I'm sick of hiding. As long as we're in this country, we'll never be safe, so I'll fight for you. Even if I have to kill... If that's what it takes for you to finally be free, I'll *fight*."

She shook her head, then she lightly butted heads with him, pressing her forehead to his brow. They locked eyes mere centimeters apart, and her sapphire irises hummed with rousing resolve.

"*No*," she seemed to say. "*We'll fight together.*"

She kissed him this time, injecting him with her undying strength. Their iron chair creaked, and what began as pecking and petting evolved into furtive groping and licking. The second they touched solid ground again, they virtually jogged to Trish's car and raced off the fairgrounds. Yumi swivelled in the passenger's seat to peer out the back window at the dwindling lights. A sudden red flare illuminated her face. Another gaudy star burst, and sparks streaked through the dark. On the mainly empty road, Ken slowed down so he could safely stroke her legs and watch the fireworks, too. As they entered the woods, the last flare fizzled against the sky like a lit matchstick.

Ken weaved through the trees, as Yumi lapped at his neck. He jerked the wheel, avoiding the ditch. She inhaled his scent, and her hand vanished underneath her skirt, and she panted, hitting his ear with long blasts of hot air. Ken veered off the dirt road and parked tucked between bushes and branches. Yumi climbed into the backseat and literally tore off her dress. Tattered bits of blue fabric drifted through the car, but Ken hesitated to move. Yumi suddenly clutched his collar and heaved him into the backseat with her like a duffle bag. Disorientated, he lay on her, ogling her flesh through the holes in her shredded dress, yet he didn't touch her, seemingly afraid to defile her faultless body. She wrapped her legs around him and squeezed, crushing his hardening cock against her damp crotch.

Yumi's legs clamped down on him like crocodile jaws, and she twisted Ken onto his back. She gripped his throat and kissed him viciously, stuffing her tongue into his mouth like a gag. He fought for air, sipping oxygen through his nostrils, as she ripped his shirt off in frayed ribbons. A blend of shame and excitement brewed inside his brain. He struggled beneath her, but she pinned his wrists to the seat and licked his face. She lashed him like that until his skin glistened with gooey saliva.

Abruptly she slid out of the vehicle and beckoned him deeper into the woods. He instinctively chased her, shedding the dangling threads of his shirt like snake skin. The humid air caressed his bare chest. Yumi deftly weaved through the brush like a sewing needle, and he followed her tail through the shadows, crunching twigs beneath his shoes. Soon they emerged on a grassy hill overlooking the lake. The white sickle moon shone below them on the glassy water and above Yumi like a halo. Blue stars seemingly swirled around her, and she glanced back at him, ghostly feral. Without breaking her gaze, she crouched onto all fours and presented herself to him, lifting her tail to unveil her slick pink lips.

"*I want you,*" her eyes said. "*I need you. I love you. If you feel the same, here I am...*"

Ken fearlessly stepped toward Yumi. Somehow, the idea of fucking in the forest like animals didn't seem so strange. Seeing her in the wild without restrains or boundaries, he felt primal, brave, and free. He kicked off his shoes and pants, marched up behind her, and kneeled. His impatient dick twitched in the wind. He tapped the tip against her mound, and she suddenly slammed her hips into him, driving him inside her like a nail. A shock of pleasure shot through his spine, and he recoiled. She followed him backward, forced him to the ground, and sat on his lap. He pierced up through her, skewering her like a rapier, and as she began to bounce, he seized her waist, paralyzed by ecstasy.

He pressed down on her silky thighs, and she clamped down on his rigid cock. He cupped her perky breasts, and her erect nipples poked through his fingers. Leaves and needles rustled nearby. The only other sounds surged from their lungs and squelched between their legs. Yumi swiveled to kiss Ken. She nipped at his lips, and their tongues tangled, their ragged breath mixed. Embracing her from behind, he stirred and churned her warm insides. His whole lap tingled, as she rotated her hips, and his cock convulsed, but just before he burst, she spun round and tackled him to the grass. Lapping at his face again, she twisted him into her slot like a screw, and then she sat upright and paused.

Moonlight rimmed her head and illuminated the sparkling teardrop on her face. Yumi smiled radiantly, brushing black strings away from her sapphire eyes, and kissed Ken. He lavishly petted her, combing her messy hair, and licked the single salty tear off her face.

Next, he linked his hands behind her back, fastened his grip, and stabbed upward once, then twice, then too fast to count. She vibrated and squeaked, clenching her teeth, and violently thrust her hips forward, as if trying to touch her navel to her chin.

They panted, and their genitals loudly collided, shooting echoing claps across the lake. Ken pounded her pussy so ferociously, the jolt nearly lifted her off his dick, so he yanked her closer after each stab. Yumi crashed her full weight down on his steely mast and stamped him into the soft earth, and her jiggling ass slapped his aching balls. She whimpered, as intense heat brewed inside her, and he growled, as her hot walls crushed his flexed flesh, and they struck their climaxes together.

Ken's cock gushed and pulsed, and Yumi's cramped hole wrung it dry, leaking clear then milky fluid. Yumi howled, firing a long clear blast at the moon, and Ken grunted and shuddered under her, until their involuntary spasms stopped. The mismatched lovers melted into a naked heap on the hill, drained, though they didn't hike back to their abandoned car until almost an hour later.

They wheeled up to the cabin, triggering the alarms. Ken expected Trish to bash through the door and scream at him over the shrieking speakers for leaving her stranded and defenceless all day. Guilt rinsed the lingering lust from his brain. He deserved whatever insult or assault she prepared, but when he imagined her foot crashing into his already chafed crotch, goose bumps broke out over his bare chest. He climbed out the car and up the porch, as if approaching the gallows. Yumi followed close, blocking her nudity behind his back. Ken peeked through the window into the lit cabin, but he couldn't spot Trish. She may have been in the washroom, bedroom, or behind the front door, waiting to ambush him with a frying pan. He swallowed hard and anxiously entered the cabin.

"Sorry, sis!" he squealed, pre-emptively flinching. No reaction. "Trish?" He scanned the silent den. The bathroom and bedroom doors hung ajar, but the bath and bed were empty. Panic attacked him, and he swept through the cabin like a brisk breeze. Trish was gone, but so was all her luggage. Yumi found the letter on the counter, but unable to read it, she passed the note to Ken.

"Dear asshole," the letter began. *"Thanks for stealing my car. I hope you find your sex slave, but I can't live like this anymore. I ordered a taxi out of here. Don't try to find me. I want nothing to do with you or your pet porn star. You ruined my life. I can't go back home. I can't go back to work. If anything happens to me, it's all your fault. But for some dumbass reason, I still love you. So please don't die."*

"Sorry, sis," Ken repeated, discarding the note. Yumi hugged him from behind. "She's right, though. We can't live like this anymore. Pack your stuff," he said, turning to smooch his doting mod. "We're going home."

CHAPTER EIGHT

"You can't own love..."

Ken and Yumi noisily pushed into their apartment and dumped their luggage at the door. Blue sunlight filtered through the airtight plastic sheets construction workers used to patch the huge hole Chopper smashed in the wall. Their home appeared otherwise untouched, preserved in its panicked state. The broken coffee table slumped beside its severed leg, and the crusty knife Ken used to stab Chopper slept on glass shards by the busted TV. Clothes and blankets lounged across the overturned bed like ghosts passed out after a rowdy party. The food inside the refrigerator also spoiled, judging by the way Yumi crinkled her nose and cringed when she neared the kitchen.

"Welcome home," Ken sighed, moving to straighten up. Somewhat surprisingly, Yumi helped. As he emptied the fridge and tidied the bedroom, she scrubbed rusty bloodstains out of the carpet. He remembered the week he adopted her, when she ripped his clothes, chewed through his pillows, and barely glanced his way. Now whenever their eyes met, her lips twitched into a subtle smile.

Perhaps the chaos of the apartment triggered memories of fighting to live and love, because the moment they finished picking up the pieces, they hopped into the shower and had sex under the hot, artificial rain. Ken no longer imagined masks or chains whenever he kissed or touched Yumi, and she rarely submitted to him, preferring to pin and ravage him on top. For their first few days back home, they affectionately assaulted each other whenever the mood struck them, but the zealous lust coursing through their bodies couldn't completely repel the demonic hounds haunting their minds.

Ken kept the puppy training alarms from the cabin and purchased a few more. He aimed an array of sensors at their front door and fire escape, and after dark, he pointed one toward the sealed hole in the living room, in case Chopper ever scaled the building and tore through the tarps.

"I'm scared, Yumi," he admitted one night. They relaxed on the couch, as raindrops pelted the plastic sheets. "I just stay awake for hours listening for those alarms, ready to fight for our lives."

Resting on his lap, Yumi flipped onto her back and blinked up at him, with a concerned pout. He patted her head, and she purred, tucking back her sharp ears.

"I know they'll come back for you," he said, massaging her scalp. "I know we'll have to confront them, but the scary thing is, I'm almost looking forward to it. I'm afraid of what we're becoming."

Yumi hugged his waist, burrowing her nose near his navel.

"I never wanted to kill somebody until I met those monsters," he said, embracing her head. "I've never wanted to hurt anyone this badly, and I keep thinking about the time you fought Chopper. You just... transformed. But is that the only way to fight a monster? To become one yourself?"

She couldn't answer, but she squeezed him tight, nuzzling and tickling his abdomen.

"I'll do anything to protect you," said Ken. "Like I said before, I'd kill and die for you, but there has to be another way. I don't want to lose you, but I don't want to lose my humanity—or yours."

Tugging her face out of his stomach, she gazed up at him sweetly.

"Promise me you won't lose yourself," he said strictly. "You're not an animal. Not like Chopper. Besides, if you overheat again... If you have another heart attack, I..." He gulped, and his eyes burned. "I don't know what I'd do without you."

Yumi smothered Ken and tumbled with him deeper into the couch, yanking him on top of her. She wrapped her limbs around him and licked his face, and her tail beat the cushions like a wooden bat. Ken licked her back, tentatively at first, then heavily enough to hear the fine hairs on her cheeks bristle on his tongue. He sank into her warm flesh, but she squirmed out from under him and lured him toward the bedroom, where she loved him like the moon might soon crash into the earth.

Ken donned his white chef uniform for the first time in a month, tied up his tiny ponytail, and went back to work the morning the restaurant reopened. His menial job helped numb his sense of dread. The dull roar of clattering dishes and chattering guests drowned out his thoughts and blunted the anxiety stippling his brain, but despite his familiar surroundings, obvious absences reminded him how much his life had changed.

While his grill sizzled and scorched, he repeatedly glanced toward the swinging kitchen door, expecting Max to reemerge at any moment. Trish's ghost distracted him even more. Every time he heard a raucous woman from the dining room, he recalled her forceful kiss.

Every time a customer complained, he resisted spitting on their food in her honour. Every time he glimpsed the redheaded belle they bought to replace Max, he remembered how the little mod saved his big sister.

He worried about her so intensely, only the scent of burning meat destroyed his daydreams. After he burned his third steak, he took an emergency break to call her and dispel his doubts.

"Don't try to find me," her letter said, but even if she wanted nothing to do with him or Yumi, Ken figured she would at least want her car. However, after three calls, she didn't pick up.

"Why aren't you answering?" he grumbled, hearing her voicemail again. He dialed her another eight times before returning to the line, where he cooked and muttered in mad bursts.

Rough memories spawned extra stress, but Yumi eased his labour. She guarded Ken at the restaurant every day and dutifully patrolled the perimeter, always available for kisses or massages during his breaks. Some guests assumed she protected the business from future attacks, but others found her suspicious and warned management about the beautiful beast wandering the parking lot. Management knew Ken owned Yumi, and they didn't mind her loitering, until customers complained. Within a few days, the owner gave him an ultimatum.

"So here's the thing," Ken told Yumi, as they left work one overcast evening. "I appreciate you being here. Honestly, I'd probably have a nervous breakdown if you weren't around," he said, holding her hand while they strolled. "But the owner doesn't like you...*bothering* customers, as he put it."

Yumi glared back at the restaurant, as though the building whispered an insult in her ear.

"That said, I wouldn't feel safe leaving you alone all day, and I'm sure you feel the same way. Besides, being my bodyguard can't be much fun. I'm surprised you don't pass out from boredom."

She shrugged bashfully, as if to say, *"Maybe I do..."*

"So, I mentioned maybe you'd like to work there," said Ken. "Not as a slave, obviously. Well, technically as a slave," he mumbled. "But because I own you, I'll get paid almost double what I make now, so you'll basically be getting paid, too. This way, we can always be together— and you can do something other than stare at traffic all day. So, what do you say? Do you want to work with—?"

Yumi suddenly hugged him, knocking him off balance. They swayed like tipping bowling pins, slow dancing, until she locked him into a secure squeeze and pecked his neck appreciatively.

"I've never seen anyone so happy to get a job before," he chuckled. "So, before we hit the park, should we go tell our boss the good news?"

She clutched his wrist and sprinted back to restaurant with him, tugging him along like a toy dog on a leash. Ken spoke to the owner inside for less than ten minutes, as Yumi giddily nodded beside him, before they reemerged with a cleaned, pressed maid outfit. Yumi held the garment against her chest. The frilly skirt barely crossed her waist, and the lacy cups looked flat. She glowered at Ken, as though he had bribed management to lend her the tiniest costume they had in stock.

"You're six feet tall," he stated. "What did you expect?"

She looked at the delicate dress like an eviction notice and hung her head.

"Maybe we can get one tailored to your...height," he said carefully. "Until then, at least you'll be popular with customers."

And she was, from the minute she shyly padded into the dining room. Every eyeball swivelled toward the tall supermodel tiptoeing between tables. She pouted and blushed, yanking her short skirt down over her panties and hoisting her cups up over her nipples, but she couldn't completely cover one without exposing the other, so she forever teetered halfway over the edge of overflowing.

Visibly nervous, she fretted despite her simple job. It didn't matter that she couldn't speak or read; she only needed to understand the numbers and colours corresponding to her section that day. Guests wrote their orders down on paper slips that she delivered to the kitchen. Some minutes later, a cook might shout, "Yumi, Blue, Four," and she would fetch the appropriate meals for that table.

Still, she dreaded approaching men, who ogled her brimming body at every opportunity. She shrank under all the attention at first, sometimes hiding in the kitchen with Ken and the other mods for minutes, yet customers forgave her slow service and showered her with smiles and compliments.

It helped that she clumsily brushed men with her tail, and that she inadvertently pushed her breasts together whenever she twisted her fingers in her lap, and that her black and white costume seamlessly blended into her silky fur, but women also treated her with common courtesy, something she never expected from strangers.

They even said, "Thank you." Up until she worked at À La Mod, she only ever heard those words from Ken.

Whenever she felt overwhelmed, she recharged with a long hug and kiss with Ken, and then ventured back to the dining room. She nervously dawdled in the beginning, but by the end of her first work week, she assertively strutted through the aisles. The attention that once frightened her now bolstered her confidence, and she proudly flaunted her beauty.

After every meal, when she brought guests their bills, she batted her eyelashes, cupped her hands into a bowl, and bent over to display her cleavage, wordlessly begging for tips. Some shooed her away, but many men took the bait, hypnotised and enamoured, and dropped a few dollars into her palms. She might have felt ashamed, but if she had to wear the stupid costume, and if men were going to leer at her anyway, she figured she would reclaim her body and make the fools pay. Besides, it felt good to take advantage of someone else for once.

Ken, however, saw things differently. When he caught her seducing a man during his break, he literally and immediately pulled her outside.

"What're you doing, huh?" he scolded her gently. "Flirting with other guys for tips? I thought you were better than that. After everything you've been through, how can you...*sell* your looks?"

Yumi folded her arms and snorted.

"I get that the slutty maid costume is a bit much, but you don't have to play the part—"

Yumi slapped him hard enough to make him stumble, but before he fell, she gripped his collar, yanked him close, and kissed him roughly.

"I know you're loyal to me," Ken mumbled against her lips. "And I'm not saying you're a..." he trailed off, recalling her spat with Trish. "I just don't like you showing yourself off like that. A lot of guys who eat here are probably *into* mods, and some might think you're... you know...asking for it."

Yumi flashed her claws and laughed, as if to say, "*I can handle any man.*"

"Right. Anyway, it's your body," he said, heading back inside. "Do what you want with it."

Ken complained now, but that night, he certainly didn't mind her playing the role of the slutty maid, and he loved what Yumi did with her body. Aside from their rare arguments—and the endless fear that a walking weapon could ambush them at any time—they lived peacefully. They worked and slept together day and night, settling into a pleasant domestic life, though they acquired unpleasant hobbies. Ken obsessively researched mod biology and the laws surrounding murder in self-defence. Yumi excessively exercised, even in bed, where she squatted and lifted wherever possible. And after work, they always visited the same crowded dog park where they previously spread their scent.

After sweating in the kitchen all day, Ken removed his chef jacket, stripping to his undershirt, and waved it like a flag. Yumi exercised as usual, running sprints from tree to tree or leisurely jogging the perimeter. From a certain bench, Ken could see every corner of the square park. He watched her run, looking for unmarked trucks, until she grew tired. She wobbled to him, fur matted with sweat.

"Maybe you shouldn't run so much," he said, patting the empty spot beside him on the bench. "All this training won't mean anything if you're exhausted when they show up."

Too fatigued to reply, she flopped across the bench and his lap. She panted rapidly, and heady pheromones wafted off her body, and her damp maid costume clung to her skin wherever her hair was thin enough. Somehow, it didn't seem appropriate for her to be in public. Ken glanced about the park, checking for children or their concerned parents. Nobody nearby appeared to care, unless they politely diverted their eyes, though a few dogs stopped to gawk at Yumi. Just to be safe, Ken refrained from stroking her, despite the temptation.

"So, I looked into it," he told her quietly, "and as long as Chopper attacks me, you can go wild. Mods can legally kill other mods to defend their owners, but you *cannot* attack Breeder," he said. "You can't attack any human, no matter how inhuman they might be—and you can't attack first. The police can pretend they can't find Chopper, but the law isn't on our side. If a judge decides you're dangerous, you'll be put down, so only attack if we're attacked first. Got it?"

Yumi mustered the energy to nod, though she looked somewhat exasperated.

"Breeder is a pathetic coward," Ken stated. "He'd never come after us alone. I'll try reasoning with him, but killing his pet would be the quickest way to end this. Hopefully you won't have to fight at all," he said, petting her fur to satisfy his urges, "but if you do, you won't fight alone."

Time ticked on tortuously, as Ken and Yumi constantly checked over their shoulders, peeked through windows, and watched the streets, but one week passed uneventfully, and another, and they started devoting less time to survival and more to living.

Ken quit studying self-defence and spent his free time caring and cooking for Yumi, and she swapped her fitness regimen for home schooling. Ken taught her to recognize those bizarre symbols called letters, and how to bark basic words she couldn't gesture with her head or hands. She slurred the words badly—understandably, with her thick long tongue—but guests at the restaurant found it especially endearing whenever she asked, "Yummy?"

They retained one habit, however: every evening, they played and relaxed at the dog park. Placing priority on living expenses, they couldn't afford to replace the television/computer destroyed during the home invasion. Ken knew Yumi loved nature, but since they couldn't afford to rent a cabin on their own either, they relegated to the city green space.

Trish hadn't contacted them since she left that letter, so Ken and Yumi still used her car. Instead of walking to the park all sweaty and tired after their shifts, they often freshened up at home before driving there. Sometimes they tossed and kicked a ball around, but today they strolled across the cloudy, verdant grounds, watching families frolic with their pets. Ken wore jeans and a buttoned white shirt. Yumi paired her favourite black leather vest with a short purple miniskirt.

All appeared peaceful, perfect.

Ken heard the panicked screams first, oblivious to the unmarked truck tearing into the park. Abrupt and alarming as an earthquake, their dreamlike interlude erupted. People and pets scattered like snowflakes in a blizzard, as the unmarked truck tore through picnic spreads and ripped ruts into the grass. It accelerated at Ken and Yumi. Suddenly the truck veered, rumbling to a clumsy stop, and the exhaust pipe rudely coughed on them, choking them with brown smoke.

Yumi recoiled at the stench of pollution, but Ken defiantly squinted into the stinging cloud, too brave or terrified to balk.

"Stay close to me," he said, grabbing her warm hand and stroking his thumb over her bumpy pads. "I'll try to talk him down. Don't fight him if you don't have to, but if Chopper charges, be ready. Remember, wait for him to attack first."

Yumi coughed, "*'Kay.*"

"His skull is like a steel helmet, and his muscles are too thick to dig through. Go for his throat," he added coolly. "You're faster, but he's got enough stamina to fight for hours, so finish him quick."

"*'Kay!*" Yumi barked, gripping his hand. He squeezed back, to tense his trembling fingers.

The truck's back door rumbled upward, as its engine cut and the smoke cleared. Through the thinning screen, Chopper's hulking silhouette took shape. A growl penetrated the fog, then something soft and heavy slammed to the ground. Chopper hopped down after the lump—*Bwoom!*—shaking the soil beneath Ken's shoes, then the beast carelessly tossed the soft bundle at Ken's feet.

Ken suffocated and panted all at once, and his lungs and eyes burned, as his heart froze solid. Trish wriggled beneath him, gagged and bound with rope, bruised and nude. His gaze drifted across her chafed auburn crotch and the bite marks on her breasts. Numb and deaf, he didn't feel the brisk breeze scrape his misty eyes, or hear Yumi whimper through her bared teeth. He stared vacantly at Trish. Her lusterless emerald glare burrowed into his pupils to scratch his brain. "*If anything happens to me, it's all your fault,*" her letter said. She scowled at Ken, then at Yumi, consuming the rest of the rage fuelling the dying fire in her soul. The flame finally flickered out. Her eyes softened and leaked, silently begging for mercy.

Ken scrambled down to free Trish, but she convulsed and squealed into her sodden rag, and when he touched her sweaty skin, an invisible blaze engulfed his cramping hand, and he instinctively leapt away. Trish gargled and writhed, flipping her bushy ginger mane back to unveil the black and yellow shock collar clamped around her neck. She stopped twitching and started sobbing. Chopper averted his gaze, adjusting the bandages over his scabs and the canvas tarp around his waist.

"Hands off, boy," said a flamboyant voice. "She isn't yours yet."

Ken and Yumi swivelled toward the demon in the metal mask. The Breeder leisurely rounded the truck and menacingly brandished the torture switch in his gloved hand. His brown trench coat billowed in the wind, revealing the stun gun and stun baton strapped to his belt. Ken recognized the police weapons, but that fact hardly registered. As he stared into the shady eyes of the chrome hound, only two words echoed inside his dark, hollow thoughts: *Die... Kill... Die. Kill. Die! Kill!*

"W-what did you do to my sister?" he growled.

"Isn't it obvious?" Breeder giggled, brushing his thumb over her shock collar trigger. "Though I'm not entirely to blame for her...wear and tear. Chopper's been rather lonely without you, Nayela," he said, ogling her up and down. "As have I. My other girls just don't compare, and human women..." he tailed away, contemplating Trish. "Well, I don't really have any other women to compare her to, but she just didn't have the same... *enthusiasm*."

"W-why?" Ken wondered, clenching his fist so hard his fingernails nearly punctured his palm. "Trish never did anything to you. She had nothing to do with this! Why would you hurt her?"

"Plenty of reasons—but can I tell you a story?" the man replied. "See, when Chopper tracked your scents to this...chubby slut, I was disappointed, to say the least. But then I realized all the things I could do with her. I could finally feel inside a real woman. I could help you *understand* the way I feel about you and Nayela. Best of all, I could get even with you. I'd say we're even now, wouldn't you?"

Ken glanced at Yumi, as though she could translate the madman's ramblings, but she stared down at Trish, even more speechless than usual, letting gravity drag the tears down her cheeks.

"How does kidnapping and torturing my sister make us even!?" Ken roared.

"Oh? You mean you don't like it when another man steals someone important to you?" asked Breeder. "You don't like it when he fucks your girl and hides her from you? As I said, we're even now. So, I'll give you your sweet sister back, and you'll give me my Nayela. An even trade, don't you agree?"

"You wanna make a deal?" Ken scoffed, quietly laughing and crying at the same time. "It's too late for that. Honestly, I was hoping to bargain with you," he said, vibrating with adrenaline. "But now, I'm glad I get to kill you."

Chopper gave a short snort, harmonizing with his owner's chuckle.

"Kill me?" asked Breeder. "How? We're not at your apartment this time. There are no knives here, no little windows to scurry through or pods to whisk you away. I made sure of that."

"You think you've got us trapped here, huh?"

"Don't I? We're in an open field. You can't hide. You can't run. You can't win. Now, I'm playing nice. You and your sister can go home and live happily ever after. All you need to do is give me back what's mine, and I'll do the same. It's a simple decision, really."

"But it's not mine," Ken said, gazing at Yumi. She glanced up from Trish, and they locked eyes. "Yumi... If you want to trade yourself for Trish, I won't stop you," he said carefully. "If that's how you want to end all this, you're free to make your own decision—but so am I!"

Ken pecked her lips and inexplicably unbuttoned her vest, peeling the leather off her breasts. Breeder and Chopper gawked at him, dumbfounded, as the sound of swords sliding from scabbards split the air. Ken tugged two long kitchen cleavers out of the sheaths stitched to the inside of her vest, then spun round. Yumi didn't bother to button her clothes. Perhaps she felt more ferocious that way, or maybe she bared herself out of guilt, in savage atonement for Trish's state.

Ken flourished his blades, sharpening them against each other—*Shhing! Shhing! Shhing!*

"Knives?" asked Breeder. Chopper shifted restlessly. "So, you planned for this."

"That's right. If you came here thinking you'd catch us off-guard, think again," said Ken. "You wanna trade?"

he asked, pointing a knife at Breeder. "How about my freedom for your life?"

"You'd rather go to prison for *murder* than let me take that whore back home?"

"Like I said, she can go home with you if she wants. That's her decision," Ken said firmly. "But for what you did to Yumi... For everything you've done to Trish, I will kill you! That's *my* decision!"

Ken recklessly launched forward, knives slicing through the air like jet wings.

"*GWOAR!*" Chopper bowled forward like an avalanche, nearly trampling Trish, and swung his fist at Ken like a hammer at a nail. Yumi suddenly darted before her lover. Chopper hesitated to crush her, halting his assault, then she hopped on his hand, scrabbled up his arm like a spider, and speared his throat. Blood sprayed her breasts and face, but she missed his windpipe. She tried to push her claws deeper into his neck, but her hand wouldn't budge. Chopper pinned her arm between his chin and shoulder, flexing his neck and chuckling, as if to say, "*I've got you now, Nayela!*"

He grasped for her, as she chomped his nose and tore off a hunk of meat. He chucked her aside and wailed, cupping his spurting face. Yumi tumbled roughly, and her sandals shot off her furry feet. She dug her toenails into the dirt and scratched through the grass, skidding to a stop.

"*Hrraugh!*" Ken bellowed, bringing his blades down on Breeder—*CLANG!* Sparks flew, as the edges etched scars into his mask. Breeder leapt back, tucking the shock collar switch into his pocket and tugging the stun baton off his belt. He gripped the rubber handle and activated the insulated tube. Blue electricity danced along the tip, hissing like a den of agitated snakes.

"Don't let her get away!" Breeder shrieked at Chopper. "Bring her back alive!"

"Take care of Chopper!" Ken called to Yumi. "I'll save Trish!"

He blitzed Breeder, carving another silver slash into his metal face. Breeder lunged, sticking Ken's shoulder— *Bzzzt!* The rod singed his shirt and paralyzed his arm, so his hand flopped open and one blade dropped. Ken ignored the small blaze sizzling at his skin and slashed Breeder—*"EYAH!"*—painting a scarlet line across his chest, then he stabbed for his heart—*Clunk!*—chipping his sternum instead. The point sank into the unfeeling bone, but before Ken could free his knife, Breeder smashed his baton into his stomach—*BZZZT!*

Acid lightning shot through Ken's veins, boiling his flesh and organs. He would have vomited, if his throat hadn't cramped shut. He desperately slashed out— *CLINGK!* The knife and baton clashed, and the bleeding, trembling foes separated to glower quietly and intensely at each other. Fiery pain replaced the numbness in Ken's dead arm. Breeder coddled his wounds, rasping through his slit.

"You can't win," he repeated. "Even if you manage to kill me, Chopper will rip you to pieces."

"Yumi will protect me," Ken stated, patting out the ember on his shoulder. "I might go to jail, but in the end, she'll finally be free. Yumi will survive! She will win!"

"Her name is NAYELA!" Breeder screeched, dashing at Ken.

Meanwhile, Chopper clumsily chased after Yumi like a toddler waddling after an elusive frog. She nimbly hopped out from between his fingers, as he ripped up handfuls of earth like an excavator, plowing the field with claws as large as garden spades. Frustrated, he *thwacked* Yumi. She sailed like a hawk skimming a lake, then *smashed* spine first into a thick tree trunk. Falling leaves rustled over her limp body. Chopper might have caught her if he rushed her now, but he inexplicably waited. He actually appeared relieved when she stood up, but then he charged, offering no further respite.

Yumi scrambled up the tree like a squirrel, as his footsteps shook more leaves off the wood. The rough bark chafed the pads on her palms, but her claws clung to it easily, so she swiftly reached the top. Chopper grabbed a branch and hoisted himself up after her—*Snap!*—but the bow instantly broke under his weight, and he fell hard onto his back—*"Ooph!"* If the situation wasn't so grim, Yumi might've giggled at him, but her budding smile bloomed into a shocked gasp, as Chopper suddenly hurtled at her like a cannonball. He seemed to hover at the peak of his jump, and they locked eyes. He swiped for her—*C-crack!*—ripping off a fistful of branches. Yumi leapt across the canopy, grasping and dangling helplessly from a sagging limb like an ornament. Chopper landed hard, quaking every leaf on the tree, then he shot at her again. Luckily her weak branch *snapped*, and he overshot her, catching only plants. She caught a sturdier branch and swung inward to dodge him on the way down. Chopper gazed up at her forlornly, clutching his twigs like a bouquet of flowers.

For a moment, it appeared as though he'd given up. Yumi feared he might bolt at Ken, and she prepared to scamper down and race Chopper there. Instead, he tossed his twigs aside, stepped back, and clenched his fist into a giant, jagged boulder. Yumi heard his muscles tighten over his knuckles. Suddenly he dashed at the tree, wound up, and threw his full strength and weight into one terrifying punch—*K-KRACK!* The trunk exploded into splinters, and the tree collapsed, creaking like a rusted hinge. Chopper waited beneath Yumi, as she tipped toward him, but just before she fell into his open hands, she leaped into the sky. The canopy smothered Chopper. He squinted through the branches, blinded, as she speared through the leaves and smashed her fist into his eyeball—*SQUITCH!*

"*UWAARGH!*" Chopper reeled back. She balanced on his broad shoulders, hammering his face. Blood squirted from his eye socket, but his rock-hard bones bruised her hand, so she hopped off him, nursing her possibly broken knuckles. Chopper seethed, forcing both eyes open. One leaked crimson and drifted sideways, dripping onto his scabs so they glistened like giant rubies imbedded in his skin. However, he didn't appear as anguished as he did absolutely irate.

In one furious motion, he grabbed the fallen tree trunk and swung it like a bat. The shattered log *crashed* into Yumi. Wooden daggers punctured her hip and shoulder, and she yelped, skipping across the field like a stone across a pond. After she finally rolled to a stop, she heaved the foot long splinter out of her thigh and screamed. Warm blood dyed her white patches red. She struggled to her feet, but the second she stood, a park bench flew at her out of nowhere. She turned to dodge, but the bench burst against her back, scattering into frayed planks and knocking her face down into the grass. Footsteps rumbled against her cheek. Chopper wiped his dead eye, steadily approaching, but she'd escaped his pursuit on a wounded leg before. She rose through the pain, wheezing through gnashed teeth.

While she fought for freedom, her lover and tormentor circled each other, just close enough for their weapons to kiss. Breeder's baton struck like a scorpion's poison stinger, and Ken sliced the shaft, narrowly deflecting each blow. *Ting! Ting! Bzzzt!* The tips touched. Electricity strangled Ken's blade, and little lightning bolts hopped onto his fingers to tickle his hand. Boldly, he grabbed the baton and lunged like a viper, impaling Breeder's coat, but only grazing his ribs. Breeder snatched his wrist, and the two men tussled briefly, before he smashed his steel snout into Ken's nose—*Crunch!*

Ken recoiled. Pain pierced his face, and blood trickled into his split lip—and then something chomped his shoulder, chewing his flesh. He twitched away from the searing teeth, staggering out of their reach, and although his agony dissolved, he couldn't feel his arm anymore. It dangled impotently at his hip. His hand hung flaccid and empty, and his knife sank into the grass under Breeder's boot.

"Well, that's anticlimactic," said Breeder. "It was a good effort—valiant, really—but unless you've got another knife stashed away somewhere, it's about time we say goodbye. Any last words, boy?"

Ken refused to show fear, clenching his jaw to keep his teeth from chattering.

"I can still fight," he replied, massaging the numb nerves in his arm.

"You're unarmed," Breeder laughed, tapping his foot on the knife. "Literally."

"Then I'll fight barehanded. I'll fight *one-handed* if I have to, but I won't give up on Yumi!"

"That's all very noble, but I'm bored of your bravado," he said, strolling forward. Ken backed away, quivering. "Now, here's what's going to happen: first I'm going to paralyze your legs; then I'm going to shock your balls until they *pop*; then, your eyes. Should I keep going? Or do you get the idea?"

"YUMI!" Ken panicked, too afraid to take his eyes off the enemy. "Help, Yumi!"

"I thought I told you," Breeder started, flourishing his baton. Blue sparks burst like fireworks. "Her name is—!" He paused, distracted by something unseen. "You!"

Ken panted, petrified and perplexed, but when he checked behind him, he noticed Trish. She shed a web of shredded ropes and yanked the gag rag out of her mouth, wielding one long blade.

"My other knife?" Ken mumbled excitedly. "When did she...?"

"You're dead," Trish stated, stomping at Breeder. He flinched at her vicious glare, stepping off of Ken's weapon. "You're dead!" she repeated, jiggling as she marched, though somehow her nudity seemed brutal and natural, like that of a mother bear storming from the forest to protect her cub. "You're fucking *dead!*"

She barrelled at Breeder, as he fumbled through his pockets for her collar trigger. He whipped it out—too late. She slashed, and he instinctively blocked, so she *chopped* his forearm—"*GYAAH!*" The knife stuck in the bone, like an axe in a stump. He wailed, and his baton and blood whirled across the grass. Trish raised her dagger over her head and roared, but before she dealt the final blow, Breeder activated her shock collar—*BZZZZT!*

"*HYEEEK!*" Trish squealed, clutching her choker with gnarled fingers, though she did not fall. Her squeal escalated into an irate growl, and she jittered at her rapist, but then—*Whack!*—Breeder punched her across her mouth, and she collapsed into a shivering pile of pink flesh and orange hair. She desperately tossed her knife at him, but the handle simply bounced off his chest. He *punted* her in the stomach like a dog.

"Fat fucking whore!" he spat, squeezing her shock collar trigger. Smoke wafted off her neck, and she wriggled and writhed, screaming. "I'm dead, eh? *You're* dead, you stupid cunt! You're—!"

"Die!" Ken yelled, leaping at Breeder. One hand still dangled uselessly, but the other gripped a knife. He slammed the edge down on the madman's hand— *"EYAAAGH!"*—hacking off a few fingers. The torture switch spiralled to the ground, along with chunks of knuckles and nails.

Breeder retreated, sprinting a few steps, before crumpling to his knees. He wept and whined, coddling his squirting stubs, while Ken knelt down by Trish. She embraced him firmly and urgently, suffocating him and bawling. He dropped his weapon, held her close, and cried into her mane.

"I'm sorry, sis," he whispered, caressing the rosy welts in her back. "I'm sorry. I'm so sorry..."

Steam rose from her throat. Ken glimpsed the blistered skin under her collar, but her wounds didn't look nearly as horrific as they smelled: savoury and delicious, like roasted pork.

"You need a hospital," he sniffed, digging the keys out of his pocket. "Your car's right there," he added, motioning toward the vehicle parked across the park. "Go get help. I'll finish up here..."

"*Make him pay*," she snarled, snatching the keys, and then she limped off toward the street, crossing her arms over her nipples. A woman jogged up and offered her a coat to conceal herself, and Ken realized then how many people stood around the park's perimeter. They chatted on their phones, safely and casually watching the action on the field, as if enjoying a sport. Something like resentment for them reignited Ken's rage, and his numb hand prickled, curling into a fist—

K-KRACK!

A sharp thunderclap shook him out of his musings. He swiveled toward the noise: Chopper lurked beneath a toppling tree. Yumi fell helplessly with it, but suddenly she shot out of the branches, twirled, and like a javelin, speared the giant. An enraged and agonized roar echoed across the park, filling Ken's ears, heart, and mind with dread. *She's going to die,* he thought. He didn't know why, but there was something inside Chopper's scream that told him the next time the beast got his hands on Yumi, he would crush her dead. It might have only been a hunch, but he couldn't risk being right.

Ken scooped a knife out of the grass and rushed Breeder. The whimpering rapist heard him approaching and feebly glanced back—just in time to see the shoe rising toward his face. Ken *kicked* the demon dead on the chin, punting his mask into the sky. With a clanging *thud*, the metal hound landed in the dirt between them, silently howling at the clouds.

"You f-fuck!" Breeder sobbed, vibrating like a toy poodle. "H-haven't you hurt me enough?"

"It's over!" Ken said, pointing his blade at the unmasked man. "Call off your dog, or else!"

Breeder wobbled upright, struggling to stand. Claw marks scarred his boyish face, ruining his otherwise handsome features. He ran his nails through his blond hair, resisting the urge to cry.

"It wasn't supposed to be like this," he whined, delirious from pain. "She loved me, you know. She was my first. After I won the lottery and bought her, I thought I was the luckiest man in the world. But my luck ran out. She didn't want me to touch her anymore—and then she did *this*," the blond man lamented. Using his stubs, he wiped out the water trickling through his scars, replacing it with blood. "I learned then that you can't buy love. You have to lock it up, and chain it down, and never let it go."

"You can't own love, either," said Ken. "It's something someone else keeps for you. It's wild, free, and random, like her. Like *Yumi*," he stressed her name. "Even if your monster drags her back, she'll never have love for you. Give her up. Let us live together in peace—and I'll let you live, too."

"You mean you're not going to kill me?" Breeder said gratefully.

Ken regarded him with pity and disdain. "I want to, and I probably should, but death is too good for you. I want you to rot in a cage until you *wish* you were dead. This country treats mods worse than dogs, and it might ignore what you do to them, but Trish is human. The law won't ignore her or all these witnesses who watched you *torture* my sister! Kill yourself in prison, if you want."

Breeder was blubbering now. Tears streaked down his pallid, sweaty face.

Ken could hardly look at his pathetic true form.

"Like I said," he began, anxiously gazing toward Chopper and Yumi, "it's over—*RYAGH!*"

Razors ripped through his bloodstream. All his muscles cramped, and Ken fell stiff on his back, gurgling at the overcast sky like an infant in his crib. Breeder's pitiful moans transformed into elated giggles, and he straddled his victim, waggling the device in his hand. Ken followed a wire down from the device to his chest, where two probes injected 50,000 volts into his nervous system.

Shit! Ken thought, unable to speak. *A stun gun? That's right... It was under his coat!*

"Don't talk down to me, you cocky piece of shit!" yelled Breeder. Ken only croaked. "You think you're better than me, huh? You think you're some sort of hero, lecturing me about love and *justice*? Well, I'll teach you what happens to heroes," he said, stealing the knife from Ken's cramped hand and kneeling at his side. "If I've learned anything about this world, it's that the villains always win!"

He *crashed* the blade into Ken's shoulder—"*UAAGH!*" Searing pain ripped through his nerves, and his vision flickered black and white. Breeder *twisted* the knife— "*GWUAK!*" Squelching meat and crunching cartilage echoed with Ken's screams, as the steel sank slowly deeper into the raw gash.

"How does that feel, *boy*?" Breeder breathed, licking his lips. "Do you like that?"

Ken groaned, losing consciousness. Breeder yanked the knife out of him, then he rose, stepped back for a running start, and *booted* his ribs—*Crack!*—fracturing the cage. He repeatedly punted him, smashing his toes into his stomach, until Ken curled up like a fetus and coughed gluey blood.

"Nayela is *mine!*" bellowed Breeder. "She might love you now, and you might have her heart, but her body and soul will *always* belong to me! You were right about one thing, though," he laughed, raising his weapon over Ken. "You should have killed me!" He plunged downward—

"*GRAWR!*" Yumi pounced on him, and they tumbled like bloodstained laundry in the dryer, all fur and leather and blades. Breeder sliced her ear, lopping off the tip, and she chomped into his hand, savagely shaking her head and rattling his knife into the grass. She chewed his fingers. They *crunched* between her fangs. Breeder *screamed*, wildly punching her head, but she barely flinched, drilling her icy blue leer into his brain, blending blood and bone inside her jagged, growling maw.

"You fucking WHORE!" he squealed, hammering on her fearsome eyes. "I'll fuck you bloody! I'll rape your corpse! I'll—!"

She punted his crotch, puncturing him with her toenails, then raked her claws across his face, stripping off his skin like a banana peel. He *screeched* like a cat trapped in an oven and melted into a gooey red puddle. She unclamped her jaw, allowing his mangled hand to caress his skewered penis. His other hand muffled his shrieks, hugging his shredded visage like some giant jungle spider.

Yumi looked down on him, seething. Suddenly an enormous hand plucked her like a flower.

"*GWOAAAR!*" Chopper roared in her face, blowing her fur back like a hairdryer. He *spiked* her to the ground so hard she bounced, grabbed her before she landed, then *slammed* her into the dirt again—*Crick!*

She heard and felt her ribs snap. Chopper bent to one knee, as if proposing, though not by choice. Yumi had apparently tore the tendons in his heel and behind his leg, destroying his mobility before she raced to rescue Ken, but she couldn't outrun Chopper now. He pressed down on her gently, pinning her like a mouse under a lion's paw.

"You *BITCH!*" Breeder snarled, writhing toward her like an undead slug. Red streaks dyed his yellow hair, and flaps of flesh hung off his maimed face. "*KILL* the whore! Kill her, *CHOPPER!*"

Chopper immediately obeyed. He lifted his fist above her head like a guillotine and growled—then hesitated. Yumi gazed up at him, vulnerable and dazed, eyes moist and breasts heaving.

"KILL HER NOW!" his owner barked.

Chopper didn't budge. In her final despairing moments, Yumi hypnotised him, weeping softly in fear, and pain, and regret. Her warm, fragile body vibrated beneath his palm like a weak heartbeat. A blood droplet dripped from his wounded eye and splashed her cheek, joining her stream of tears.

"N-no..." Yumi spoke, startling him slightly. "P-please... No..."

Breeder shambled at Chopper's angelic prey, dragging his feet and baton. Rage, vengeance, and bodily chemicals fuelled the savage criminal, carrying him toward Yumi like a puppet.

"Get off 'er," he muttered. Chopper didn't hear, or else he didn't listen. "I said, GET OFF!"

Breeder *jabbed* his baton into his huge hand. Chopper reacted as though a doorknob shocked him, but he removed his hand nonetheless. Breeder stood over Yumi. Blood trickled from his crotch, staining her pelt.

"She's mine," he hissed, barely clinging to the cliff of consciousness. "*I* bought her... *I* own her... *I* love her, not you! Her life is *mine!*"

He *thrust* the stun baton into her chest, jolting her heart. She gasped and howled, squirming, as the crackling tip scorched her fur like a cigar burning a black blotch into a pillow.

Her screams roused Ken. He groggily flopped onto his stomach and crawled toward her like a hobbling caterpillar, but severe vertigo from the stun gun left him immobilized and disoriented.

"Y-Yumi," he rasped, splashing in the blood that spit from his shoulder. "Yumi!"

She replied with another ear-splitting howl, jerking and juddering. Her silky fur caught fire.

"It'll all be over soon," Breeder consoled her, glistening in frigid sweat. "Die for me, darling... There you go. Just like that! Die... Die! DIE—!"

THWACK!—Chopper *smacked* his owner with the back of his hand. The Breeder bounced over the field like a marble over concrete, rolling into a twisted, crooked heap a hundred metres away.

"N-Na..." the demon whispered vaguely. "N-Nay...ela..."

Finally he slumped off to sleep, broken and alone.

Chopper tenderly scooped Yumi up like a ragdoll, and with his thumb, he smothered the small blaze licking between her breasts. The wilted flower sagged across his fingers, and her heart tapped erratically on his thumb, like a lover knocking at his door in the middle of the night. He glanced at his fallen master and scoffed, then gazed across Yumi and licked his lips. She hardly breathed, fading.

Ken could only guess what the creature was thinking. Maybe he felt his master was no longer the pack leader. Maybe he believed Yumi, the only warrior who ever challenged him in combat, was his equal. Maybe he thought he was the alpha male now, and that he had earned his beautiful prize.

Chopper's one ear perked up. Police sirens whirred in the distance, and he cupped Yumi, as if protecting a dying flame from the wind. The beast shrank away from the shrill noise, about to bolt. Ken knew that if Chopper eloped with Yumi, he'd never see or feel her again, but he was helpless to free her or even stand on his own. He could only beg like a dog whining for table scraps.

"Chop—!" Ken yelped, straining just to speak. "Chopper!"

The monster swivelled at him and paused.

"Please, let her go," he said, clutching the grass to tug himself forward. "She's suffered enough already. If you care about her—about *Yumi*—about *Nayela*... If you love that woman at all, let her be free! Let her live her own way! Doesn't she deserve that choice? Doesn't she deserve freedom?"

Chopper considered his points carefully, but the sirens made the more compelling argument. He gradually retreated, bowing ever so slightly, as if apologizing, though Ken never expected him to set her free. He only meant to stall and allow the car charging through the field to reach Chopper.

The engine growled like a tiger, and Chopper spun at the sound—too late. Trish *crashed* into his leg. The bones splintered grotesquely, stabbing up through his skin like porcupine quills. Chopper fumbled Yumi, and she flopped to the ground like a bag of sugar beside Ken. While the beast yowled and whimpered, Trish raced out of the car, parking it on top of his shattered leg. She stumbled toward her brother and sister, clasping her borrowed coat close, as if trudging through a blizzard.

"Trish?" said Ken. "You came back..."

"Are you okay?" she asked, touching the tender area around her collar.

Ken checked on Yumi before replying. She stirred, laying slanted on her hip like a mermaid.

"I think so," he said unconvincingly, unable to even sit up under his own power.

Trish gasped, as she drew close enough to notice his wound. "You *think* so? Look at your arm! I swear, I leave you alone for one sec—"

"LOOK OUT!" Ken cried, as Chopper furiously hurled her car at them like a brick.

Trish cowered under the shadow of the massive steel meteor, pointlessly shielding her face—*CRUNCH!*—but just before the vehicle squashed her, two strapping mods in uniforms caught the car, crushing the undercarriage in their claws like a crane. Half the size of Chopper, the black and brown mods worked in tandem to match his strength. They set the car down, nodded reassuringly at Trish, and then joined their pack. Six or seven mods of the same breed surrounded Chopper, snarling.

"MK9s?" Ken said gratefully.

They had sprinted ahead of the police cars that now careened onto the field, sirens blaring. Officers piled out wielding shotguns, stun batons, and riot gear, and enclosed the wounded war mod. Ken suddenly felt guilty for cursing all the spectators on their phones. If only he had known they were calling in an army instead of texting their dumb friends—though they likely did that, too.

"You're surrounded!" one cop shouted at Chopper through a megaphone. "Surrender or die!"

Chopper's eyes flited at the handsome MK9s, and he bristled, as if competing to attract a mate, but he didn't fight. Acknowledging defeat, he whimpered, lowered his ears, and rolled onto his back, displaying his scabby belly.

The MK9s attacked him anyway.

Chopper barely got the chance to defend himself. He managed to flail onto his stomach, but four police mods already gnawed on his joints, two twisted his arms behind his back, and one choked him from behind, cutting off the blood supply to his brain.

Before Chopper blacked out, Yumi approached him, breaching the ring of police. They trained their barrels on her, but after seeing how she staggered and panted, they lowered their weapons. She stopped just out of Chopper's reach, just in case he desperately held her hostage, but he only stared at her, pleading for help and whining. Yumi took a deep, calming breath.

"Than...ks," she spoke. Chopper's eyes gleamed, but not with blood. "So...rry..."

Chopper fell asleep.

Yumi shuffled back through the police line to Trish and Ken, gripping her sore chest and her trickling leg. She patted Trish on the head appreciatively, then she helped Ken stand, embraced him, and quickly licked his cheek.

Ken kissed her forehead in return, leaving rosy lip prints, as though he was wearing lipstick. She didn't have a fever.

"Is that it?" Trish asked anxiously. "Is it over?"

"Yes," Ken exhaled. "We're finally free... All of us."

Yumi smiled solemnly.

"Let's...go," she said, grasping the hands of the humans she treasured. "Home."

EPILOGUE

"You're not his pet anymore."

Two long kabobs of plump juicy shrimp sizzled on the grill. Flames licked through the black grate, charring the succulent seafood to perfection. Ken only needed to apply the finishing touches. With one hand, he flipped the skewers with tongs one last time. With the other, he reached toward a mixing bowl for the citrus sauce— *"Aaugh!"*—but pain paralyzed his arm, shooting down his shoulder.

The other chefs heard him yelp over the din of the kitchen and glanced his way.

"I'm fine, guys," Ken winced, rotating his shoulder. "My nerve's just acting up again..."

They went back to work, though he somehow felt snubbed, like they only looked because he distracted them and not because they cared. But maybe it was all in his head. It had been a long shift, and a late dinner rush had forced him to work steady for the past two hours. He longed for a break, but he needed to fulfill the orders for one more table first.

He spun back to the grill—and found Yumi. She leaned over the shrimp in her cute frilly maid costume, sniffing and moaning dreamily. Then her thick pink tongue flopped from her mouth, and in slow motion, a gooey stream of drool drooped onto the kabobs. Her spit crackled on the barbecue.

"Hey!" Ken shooed her off. "What do you think you're doing?"

Yumi batted her big blue eyes and twisted innocently.

"Okay?" she asked, and he realized she hadn't come running for the shrimp.

"Oh... You heard me yell, huh?"

She nodded, ears bobbing.

"Like I told these guys, I'm fine. Sometimes it just stings a little. Don't stress about it, all right? Here," he added, plucking a kabob off the grill by its wooden stem. "For making you worry. Also, because you ruined it..."

Yumi gleefully accepted the treat and toddled off, but rather than nibble on it alone in a corner like some greedy chipmunk, she shared it with the other serving girls, picking shrimp off the skewer like flower petals and placing them on their palms and tongues.

After firing up another round of kabobs, Ken said, "Keira, Gold, Seven!"

There was no response.

"Keira, Gold, 7?"

No reply.

"Keira!" he called impatiently. He spotted her, a young blond mod, on the opposite end of the kitchen. She shyly fidgeted with her fingernails, looking lost and overwhelmed. "Keira? KEIRA!"

Still, no reaction.

"KEI—*Ouch!*"

Trish slapped him upside the head.

"Give it a rest already!" she barked, adjusting the green scarf around her neck. "She hears you. She probably just forgot her new name."

"Well, I forgot her old one," Ken said sheepishly, "so..."

Trish cupped her mouth and shouted, "Bliss!" The blond mod looked. "Gold! Seven!"

The girl weaved through the kitchen like a child fumbling through a dark forest. She grabbed the tray of kabobs from Ken's window, then Trish patted her head and told her, "Thanks, *Keira*."

The mod gasped and blushed, realizing that Ken had been calling her, and bowed in apology.

"It's all right," said Trish. "Just remember, you don't need to use the name *he* gave you, okay? You're not his pet anymore."

Trish ruffled her golden hair, and Keira purred happily, before hurrying to the dining room. Ken's eyes followed her out, glued to the thin pink lines that scarred her fuzzy back.

"I thought it was only Yumi," Ken said, absentmindedly wiping down his station. "You know, payback for scarring his face." He glanced at a busty brunette mod with wrinkles ringing her throat. "But it looks like he tortured all his girls..."

"Stop worrying," said Trish. "The deranged asshole who hurt them is locked in a padded cell. These women are safe now—at least from The Breeder."

"I guess. I mean, it's great that they can work together and support each other and everything. I just wish we could do more for them."

"Well, you can't adopt them all," she said, secretly praying she didn't give him any ideas.

"I just didn't realize how many girls he actually owned. Did the police even find them all?"

"Probably. Breeder wasn't talking, but they used that bloodhound of his to track them down, right? I'm sure they rescued them all before they starved or whatever.

As for what they did with that monster when they were done with it..." she tailed away. "Well, it doesn't really matter, does it?"

"Yeah..." Ken said, tossing his towel on the counter.

"You look tired," Trish changed the subject. "You wanna take this outside?"

"Take this outside?" he replied. "Are we gonna talk or have a back-alley brawl?"

"Har-dee-har-*har*," she said childishly, moving to the backdoor, assuming he would follow. "Come on, I could use the fresh air."

She tossed on the winter jacket hanging by the backdoor, but Ken had sweltered over the grill all night and figured he should cool off. He met her outside on the short staircase beneath the drifting snowflakes. Steam swirled off his forehead toward the stars. He inhaled the crisp air, leaning against the wall beside the backdoor. Trish rested on the steel railing, searched her pockets, and then ignited a cigarette. She stuffed the pack and lighter away and sucked on the filter.

"Aren't you cold?" she asked, blowing smoke. White snowflakes speckled her orange mane.

"We won't be out here long," he shivered.

"Suit yourself," she said, taking another puff. "How's your shoulder, by the way?"

"For the last time," he grumbled, "it's *fine.*"

"All right! Shit," she said defensively. "Sorry for giving a damn."

Ken exhaled a stream of fog. "No, I'm sorry. Don't tell Yumi, but..." He glanced about, as though she might be spying on him. "Honestly, it's been bothering me lately. But the pain is good, in a way."

"Oh...? How so?"

"It reminds me why I fought," he answered coolly. "Every time it hurts, I'll remember what I went through for you and Yumi. I'll remember what's important, and I'll never take you for granted."

"Good," she replied. "I look forward to being appreciated for once."

"*Besides,*" he went on, "despite all the shit that happened to us, it could've been worse."

"Worse?" Trish repeated, affronted. "How could it have been *worse*, exactly?"

"Well, would you rather be dead right now?"

Trish broke eye contact, shuffling her shoes through a patch of snow. She readjusted the green scarf that matched her glistening eyes. Her pink scars peeked over the wool, and she shrugged.

"Hey..." Ken said concernedly, hugging her tight. He squeezed her puffy coat, and she clutched his chef's jacket, and their soft cheeks caressed. "I'm sorry. I love you, okay? I didn't mean it like that. I just meant—"

"I know," she sniffled. "We're still alive. We still have each other..."

"Right," he said, separating from his sister. "But I don't just mean we could've died. Honestly, it's a miracle none of us are behind bars right now."

She sniffed once more, composing herself. "All we did was defend ourselves."

"I guess," he said, "but who knows what the jury was thinking."

"I don't think any jury would've been heartless enough to convict us," she argued, "especially in Yumi's case. She would've gotten the death penalty. I mean, if you heard a girl was raped, tortured, hunted, and almost killed by some psychopath, would you sentence her to *death* for fighting back?"

"Of course not," Ken answered instantly.

"Then why do you think other people would?" she asked, dragging on her cigarette. "You can't go through life assuming everyone's an asshole. You have to have *some* faith in humanity, right?"

"I do," he claimed, "but it'll take more than one sympathetic jury to change this country,"

"Well, maybe we're on the right track. The Breeder case is getting big news coverage. Up until now, nobody really thought about sex slavery because it all happened behind closed doors, but now it's out in the open. People are talking, and I'm sure that's just the beginning. Trust me," she smiled. "Because you fought for Yumi, mods will have rights someday."

"Well, I didn't fight alone," said Ken. "I can honestly say we would be dead without you."

"True," she humbly agreed. "But in your case, that's been true since we were kids."

Ken chuckled warmly, though his teeth chattered from a chilly breeze.

"I mean it. You've really been there for all those girls inside, too. Giving them new names..."

"Well, they all had stripper names like Bliss, so..." Trish trailed off modestly.

"Getting them jobs, t-taking them out for drinks..."

"Hey, those girls had it rough. Anyone would do that for them," she said, blushing.

"H-have you th-thought about adopting?" he shivered.

She laughed at him, tapping her ashes onto the snow.

"Go get your jacket," she ordered. "Who're you trying to impress?"

"Ken?" Yumi peeped, poking through the backdoor.

"Actually, never mind," Trish said, pre-maturely extinguishing her cigarette beneath her heel. "I'm heading back inside. I'll let you two have some alone time."

As she squeezed past Yumi, she affectionately stroked her scruffy head and said, "Have fun..."

She shut the door behind her, giving the interspecies lovers privacy.

"Did you come to warm me up?" Ken asked, though she had already accomplished that. She lightly steamed and panted, glowing in the moonlight. Snowflakes melted against her face, accenting her beauty with tiny twinkling diamonds. Yumi bashfully approached him, and his blood rushed. She pressed him back against the railing, moistened her lips with a quick lick, and then finally kissed Ken.

He melted like a marshmallow over a campfire, tasting her savoury mouth, but suddenly she pushed off of him and teasingly retreated, twisting in and nearly spilling out of her lacy uniform.

"Wait," she spoke. "Home."

"I see," he said, intrigued. "You'll give me the rest later, huh?"

Yumi giggled, sticking out her tongue and winking.

"Fair enough," he sighed. "So, how are Blis—*er*, Keira and the other girls doing?"

"Hmm..." Yumi hesitated, then tilted her hand side to side. "So-so."

"That well, huh?" he sighed again, heavier. "Well, adjusting to people might take them time. Ophelia just got out of therapy, and Kailyn..." He paused, acutely aware of Yumi's wilting expression. "Sorry. I'm kind of killing the mood here, huh?"

"Uh-huh," she grunted.

Ken sighed once more, expelling a huge humid cloud.

"Sorry," he repeated. "I just worry about them, you know? I wish I could say it'll be okay—that they'll all find happiness the way you did—but I can't, and it bothers me so much I could *scream*. I know I can't rescue them all, but there are thousands of slaves still suffering out there, and..."

Yumi blinked at him nervously.

"Sorry," he said one last time. "Just thinking out loud..."

"Okay?" she wondered.

He gazed into her earnest, icy eyes, searching for the answer.

"I will be," he said certainly, "as long as I have you."

"You?" she squeaked sweetly. "Me? Love?"

"That's right, puppy," he said, stalking toward Yumi. She let him touch her, and they nuzzled briefly, before kissing passionately against the wall. Their tongues tapped, and their eyelashes flicked together, and their fingers entwined. Her love and lust burned within him so fiercely, he barely felt the biting wind, or the shooting pain in his arm. Ken fondled her pointed ears, caressed her furry tail, smooched her dark lips, and whispered to the beautiful beast, "You and me..."